A MANUAL OF SANSKRIT PHONETICS

In Comparison With the Indogermanic Mother-Language, for Students of Germanic and Classical Philology

MAVEN BOOKS

A MANUAL OF SANSKRIT PHONETICS

In Comparison With the Indogermanic Mother-Language, for Students of Germanic and Classical Philology

C. C. UHLENBECK

Extraord Professor of Sanskrit and comparative Philology
in the University of Amsterdam

MAVEN BOOKS

Chennai   Trichy   New Delhi

This edition has been published in india by arrangement with Carson Books, UK

ISBN 978-93-5527-353-6 **Maven Books**

All rights reserved   No. 44, Nallathambi Street,
Triplicane, Chennai 600 005

MJP 1490   © Publishers, 2023

Publisher : C. Janarthanan

Publisher's Note

The legacy of a country is in its varied cultural heritage, historical litera-ture, developments in the field of economy and science. The top nations in the world are competing in the field of science, economy and literature. This vast legacy has to be conserved and documented so that it can be bestowed to the future generation. The knowledge of this legacy is slowly getting perished in the present generation due to lack of documentation.

Keeping this in mind, the concern with retrospective acquiring of rare books has been accented recently by the burgeoning reprint indus-try. Maven Books is gratified to retrieve the rare collections with a view to bring back those books that were landmarks in their time.

In this effort, a series of rare books would be republished under the banner, "Maven Books". The books in the reprint series have been carefully selected for their contemporary usefulness as well as their historical im-portance within the intellectual. We reconstruct the book with slight en-hancements made for better presentation, without affecting the contents of the original edition.

Most of the works selected for republishing covers a huge range of subjects, from history to anthropology. We believe this reprint edition will be a service to the numerous researchers and practitioners active in this fascinating field. We allow readers to experience the wonder of peer-ing into a scholarly work of the highest order and seminal significance.

Maven Books

PREFACE.

The idea of publishing an English edition of my *Handboek der Indische Klankleer* (Leiden, Blankenberg & C°. 1894) was suggested to me by others; but for that suggestion this translation certainly would not have been undertaken. In general I have followed the Dutch text: alterations have been made only, when there were positive inaccuracies in the Dutch edition or when an alteration had become necessary because of the progress of comparative philology since 1894. I have also considerably augmented the references to the scientific literature and somewhat enlarged the part on the accent. Some emendations are due to the recensions of Kern, Speyer, Zubatý [and Johansson], of whose observations and remarks I have made a grateful use.

I further need only repeat, what I said in the preface to the Dutch original: the purpose of my having composed this little handbook is to introduce the student into the comparative-phonetic study of Sanskrit. Though as a rule students of Classical and Germanic philology do not read Vedic texts, I have not hesitated to cite words and forms, which had already become obsolete in the epic and classical language, mentioning, of course, the fact, that such a word only occurs in Vedic. In general I have avoided to cite Iranic, Lithuanian and Slavonic: I know, it is true, that this lessens the scientific worth of my book, but I do not think it desirable to trouble the student with several languages, which are either quite unknown to him or which he only just begins to learn.

May this edition be of some use to the students in England, America and India.

Amsterdam, Nov. 1897.   C. C. UHLENBECK.

CONTENTS.

PART I. SYSTEM OF VOWELS.

A. The representation of the Indogermanic vowels in Sanskrit.

B. THE RELATION OF THE INDIAN VOWELS TO THE INDOGERMANIC.

PART. II. SYSTEM OF CONSONANTS.

A. THE REPRESENTATION OF THE INDOGERMANIC CONSONANTS IN SANSKRIT.

Semivowels.

Nasals.

B. The relation of the Indian consonants to the Indogermanic.

Semivowels.

Nasals.

Liquids.

Labial explosives.

Page

INTRODUCTION.

§ 1· **The Indogermanic family of languages.** The great
family of languages, to which Sanskrit belongs, is called the
Indogermanic, Indoceltic or Aryan. I prefer the first name,
because it is the most usual, though the name *Indoceltic* may
claim a greater accuracy. The word *Indogermanic* dates from
a time, when it was not yet proved, that the Celtic dialects
also make part of our family of languages, and indicates by
the combined name of the utmost branches, Indian and Germanic, the whole territory of speech, to which they belong.
Now that it is certain, that Celtic also is a member of our
family, it would be accurate to replace the word *Indogermanic*
by *Indoceltic*, because not Germanic, but Celtic is the utmost
branch to the Occident. The name *Indogermanic* however is
generally adopted and it would be impossible to supplant it
by another. By the word *Aryan* is generally understood a
certain subdivision of the Indogermanic family, viz. the Indo-
Iranian, and therefore it would seem unsuitable to use this
name also for the whole Indogermanic family. See G. Meyer,
Idg. forschungen 2, 125 sqq. and Spiegel, Die Arische periode
(Leipzig 1887) VI sq.

The Indogermanic family consists of the following nine
groups:

1. *Aryan*, see § 2.

2. *Armenian.*

3. *Phrygian-Thracian*, only known from proper names, glosses and inscriptions.

4. *Albanian.*

5. *Greek.*

6. *Italic*, which comprises not only ancient languages of Italy (Latin, Oscian, Umbrian, Samnitic), but also the modern dialects, which have sprung from popular Latin.

7· *Celtic*, which is divided into Gallic (the extinct language of ancient Gallia), Britannian (Cymric or Welsh, Cornish, Bas-Breton) and Gaelic (Scotch, Irish, Manx).

8. *Germanic*, which is commonly divided into an eastern and a western group. The eastern comprehends Gothic and Scandinavian (Icelandic, Danish, Norwegian, Swedish); to the western belong English (in its oldest literary period called Anglosaxon), Frisian and German (High-German and Low-German)

9. *Balto-Slavonic*, which consists of two groups, the Baltic and the Slavonic. The former is divided into Old-Prussian, Lithuanian and Lettish; the latter comprehends Southern-Slavonic (Ecclesiastical-Slavonic, Slovenian, Servo-Croatian, Bulgarian), Russian (Great-Russian, White-Russian, Little-Russian) and Western-Slavonic (Polish, Wendish, Bohemian and the extinct Polabic).

About the mutual relations of these groups see J. Schmidt, Die verwandtschaftsverhältnisse der Indogermanischen sprachen (Weimar 1872) and cf. Brugmann, Zur frage nach den verwandtschaftsverhältnissen der Indogermanischen sprachen (Techmer's Internationale Zeitschr. für allgemeine sprachwissenschaft 1, 226 sqq.).

§ 2. **The Aryan group**. The Aryan group is divided into two subdivisions:

1. *Indian*, see § 3.

2. *Iranian*.

Ancient Iranian is handed down to us in two dialects, viz. Avestian and Old-Persian. Avestian is the language of the Avesta, the sacred book of the Parsis. The oldest parts of this Zoroastrian bible date back to many centuries before Christ, and their language is more archaic than the classical dialect of the younger Avesta. This oldest Avestian is called the *Gāthā*-dialect. In Old-Persian we have only the cuneiform inscriptions of the Achaemenidian kings, the oldest of which is that of Darius Hystaspes at Behistān and dates from ± 520 before Christ. Numerous inscriptions are found on and near the ruins of Persepolis: the youngest of them is of the middle of the fourth century before Christ. See Bartholomae, Handbuch der Altiranischen dialekte (Leipzig 1883), Vorgeschichte der Iranischen sprachen (Grundriss der Iranischen philologie I); Williams Jackson, An Avesta grammar (Part I, Stuttgart 1892); Spiegel, Die Altpersischen Keilinschriften [2] (Leipzig 1881).

The language of the Sassanidian period is called Middle-Persian, Pahlavī or Huzvāresh. The modern Iranian dialects are New-Persian, Kurdish, Ossetic, Afghan, Balūčī &c. Some of the principal works on these languages are: Horn, Grundriss der Neupersischen etymologie (Strassburg 1893); Hübschmann, Persische studien (Strassburg 1895), Etymologie und lautlehre der Ossetischen sprache (Strassburg 1887); Justi, Kurdische grammatik (Petersburg 1880); Trumpp, Grammar of the Paštō (= Afghan, London 1873); Geiger, Etymologie des Balūčī (München 1890), Lautlehre des Balūčī (München 1891); Tomaschek, die Pamir-dialekte (Wien 1880).

§ 3. **The Indian dialects.** In the first place is to be

mentioned the Vedic dialect, which was spoken in the Panjāb
and in Kābulistān $\pm$ 1500 before Christ. Here arose the greater
part of the *ṛc*-hymns, which in a later period, when the
Indo-Aryans had spread more to the East, were collected into
the Ṛgvedasaṁhitā. From this time dates the greater part
of the Vedic literature.

From an Indian dialect of the Veda-period sprang the *saṁskṛtā
bhāṣā* (adorned, elaborated language) of Madhyadeça (the Mid-
land, on the upper course of the Gaṅgā and Yamunā), which
some centuries before Christ must have been a living language,
be it not in quite the same form as in most of the literary
Sanskrit works. To the time, when Sanskrit was yet living
as a popular language, we may refer at least the bulk of
the great epic poems Mahābhārata and Rāmāyaṇa. There are
several reasons to assume that this spoken Sanskrit descends
from an other Old-Indian dialect than that of the Vedic hymns
(cf. § 43). The most indispensable books for Sanskrit students
are: Whitney, A Sanskrit grammar [3] (Leipzig 1896), The
roots, verb-forms and primary derivatives of the Sanskrit
language (Leipzig 1885); Wackernagel, Altindische grammatik I (Göttingen 1896); Böhtlingk & Roth, Sanskritwör-
terbuch (Petersburg 1855—1875). See also the list of books
in Lanman's Sanskrit reader (Boston 1888), XVII sqq.

While Sanskrit continued as the language of the learned
and educated, there arose numerous popular dialects or Prākrit's (*prākṛtā bhāṣā*, ordinary language), many of which are
known to us, partly from separate works, partly from Sanskrit
plays (fifth, sixth and following centuries after Christ). At
how early a time Sanskrit can no longer have been a popular
language, appears from the Prākrit inscriptions of Açoka,
king of Pāṭaliputra, who reigned from 259 till 222 before

Christ. Particularly interesting is that Prākrit, in which the sacred books of the southern Buddhists are written and which is called *Pāli*. Kern (Geschiedenis van het Buddhisme in Indië, Haarlem 1882—1884, 2, 339) says, that Pāli is a dialect, the place of which is not yet fixed with entire certainty, but that at all events it was not the language of Açoka and the kingdom of Magadha. Oldenberg (Buddha, Berlin 1881, 76) thinks, that Pāli was once the popular language of southern India. See about the ancient popular dialects of India Lassen, Institutiones linguae Pracriticae (Bonnae 1837); Jacobi, Ausgewählte erzählungen in Mahārāṣṭrī (Leipzig 1886); Ernst Kuhn, Beiträge zur Pāli-grammatik (Berlin 1875) and other works.

From these Prākrits descend the modern Aryan vernaculars of India: Hindī (intermixed with numberless Persian and Arabian words it is called Hindustānī or Urdū), Panjābī, Sindhī, Gujarātī, Marāṭhī, Oriya, Bengālī &c. See Beames, A comparative grammar of the modern Aryan languages of India (London 1872—1879).

§ 4. **Sounds and letters.** The oldest Indian writing, that is known to us, is found in the inscriptions of Açoka: here we distinguish two different systems of characters, one of which has been evidently derived from a Semitic alphabet and the other may be of the same origin. From the latter descend the younger Indian alphabets, to which belongs Devanagarī, properly the alphabet of Hindustān. The natives of India write Sanskrit in different modes, but by western scholars Devanagarī is only used.

Here I give a list of the Sanskrit letters, according to the most usual system of transliteration: each character has always the same phonetic value and all sounds of the language are represented by a separate character.

Vowels.

a, *ā*, *i*, *ī*, *u*, *ū*.
e, *o*.
ṛ, *ṝ*, *ḷ*, *ḹ*.

Diphthongs.

āi, *āu*.

Mutes.

Gutturals:	*k*,	*kh*,	*g*,	*gh*.
Linguals:	*ṭ*,	*ṭh*,	*ḍ*,	*ḍh*.
Dentals:	*t*,	*th*,	*d*,	*dh*.
Labials:	*p*,	*ph*,	*b*,	*bh*.

Palatal affricates.

c, *ch*, *j*, *jh*.

Nasals.

ṅ, *ñ*, *ṇ*, *n*, *m* and the anusvāra and anunāsika, which in transliteration are both written *ṁ*.

Liquids.

r, *l*.

Semivowels.

y, *v*.

Sibilants.

ç, *ṣ*, *s*.

Aspiration.

h and the visarga *ḥ*.

The usual order of arrangement is slightly different from that given above.

A few words must be said on the phonetic value of the Devanāgarī letters.

The *a*, *i* and *u* are short vowels: their pronunciation is nearly the same as in German. The corresponding long vowels are *ā*, *ī*, *ū*.

The *e* and *o* are long vowels with a narrow pronunciation: they are contractions of *ai* and *au*.

The *r* and *l* are sonant liquids; *r̄* and *l̄* are the corresponding long ones, but *l̄* does not occur in a single genuine Sanskrit word.

The *āi* and *āu* are diphthongs: their first component *ā* is long, the second components are the semivowels *i̯* and *u̯*.

The *k* and *g* are the ordinary European *k*- and *g*-sounds. Their corresponding aspirates are *kh* (*k* + *h*) and *gh* (*g* + *h*).

The *ṭ* and *ḍ* are distinguished from the dentals by turning up the tip of the tongue to the palate. Their corresponding aspirates are *ṭh* (*ṭ* + *h*) and *ḍh* (*ḍ* + *h*).

The *t* and *d* are ordinary dentals, i. e. they are formed by turning up the tip of the tongue to the upper teeth. Their corresponding aspirates are *th* (*t* + *h*) and *dh* (*d* + *h*).

The *p* and *b* are ordinary labials and *ph* (*p* + *h*) and *bh* (*b* + *h*) are their corresponding aspirates.

The *c* and *j* are palatal affricates: *c* consists of *t* + *ś* and *j* of *d* + *ź*. Engl. *ch* in *chaff, chain, choose, churl* and *g, j* in *gem, gentleman, gin, jail, jam, jest, jockey* are nearly the same sounds.

Each of the nasals is akin to one of the series of consonants given above: the *ṅ* is guttural (= engl. *ng* in *long, sing*), the *ṇ* lingual, the *n* dental, the *m* labial and the *ñ* palatal. By *ṁ* (anusvāra and anunāsika) is indicated the nasal pronunciation of a preceding vowel.

The *r* must have been a lingual sound, because it has the power to lingualize neighbouring dentals. The *l* is a dental sound.

The *y* is a semivowel, which is closely related to the vowel *i*; i. e. it is a consonant *i* like engl. *y* in *year, yard, yoke.* The *v* originally stood in the same relation to *u* and had the sound of engl. *w* in *wall, word, wear;* but from an early time it was changed to a spirant (engl. *v* in *veil, vain, vine*), except when preceded by a consonant in the same syllable.

The *ç* is palatal like engl. *sh* in *short, shield, shut.* The *ṣ* is lingual and distinguished from the *s* in the same way as *ṭ, ḍ, ṇ* from *t, d, n.* The *s* is our ordinary surd *s.*

By *h* and *ḥ* are understood our usual *h* (spiritus asper), but the visarga (*ḥ*) is usually neglected by us in the pronunciation of Sanskrit words.

PART I.

SYSTEM OF VOWELS.

A. The representation of the Indogermanic vowels in Sanskrit.

§ 5. **The Indogermanic vowels in general.** There was a great variety of vowels in the mother-language, but their accurate pronunciation is not definable. We indicate these vowels by the following letters:

$$a, \bar{a}; \quad e, \bar{e}; \quad o, \bar{o}; \quad \partial; \quad i, \bar{i}; \quad u, \bar{u}.$$

The e, $\bar{e}$, o, $\bar{o}$ had a broad pronunciation. The ∂ was perhaps something between a and engl. e in *oldest, father*.

There were also sonant nasals and liquids, which are written $m̥$, $n̥$, $r̥$, $l̥$. We understand by $n̥$ not only the dental n-sonans, but also the palatal and guttural sonant nasals. Some scholars deny the existence of these sounds in the mother-language: see Bechtel, Die hauptprobleme der Indogermanischen lautlehre seit Schleicher (Göttingen 1892), 114 sqq. and J. Schmidt, Kritik der sonantentheorie (Weimar 1895), cf. Hirt, Idg. forschungen 7, 147 sqq.

Combinations of vowels with semivowels, nasals and liquids were very common:

$$a\underset{\circ}{i}, \quad \bar{a}\underset{\circ}{i}, \quad e\underset{\circ}{i}, \quad \bar{e}\underset{\circ}{i}, \quad o\underset{\circ}{i}, \quad \bar{o}\underset{\circ}{i};$$

$$a\underset{\circ}{u}, \quad \bar{a}\underset{\circ}{u}, \quad e\underset{\circ}{u}, \quad \bar{e}\underset{\circ}{u}, \quad o\underset{\circ}{u}, \quad \bar{o}\underset{\circ}{u};$$

$$am, \quad \bar{a}m, \quad em, \quad \bar{e}m, \quad om, \quad \bar{o}m, \quad \partial m;$$

$$an, \quad \bar{a}n, \quad en, \quad \bar{e}n, \quad on, \quad \bar{o}n, \quad \partial n;$$

$$ar, \quad \bar{a}r, \quad er, \quad \bar{e}r, \quad or, \quad \bar{o}r, \quad \partial r;$$

$$al, \quad \bar{a}l, \quad el, \quad \bar{e}l, \quad ol, \quad \bar{o}l, \quad \partial l.$$

Many scholars assume, that there were also long sonant nasals and liquids in the mother-language. See de Saussure, Mémoire sur le système primitif des voyelles dans les langues Indo-Européennes (Paris 1887), 262 sqq. and Brugmann, Grundriss der vergleichenden grammatik der Indogermanischen sprachen (Strassburg 1886—1893), 1, 208 sq. 243 sqq.: against this theory Bechtel 203 sqq.

§ 6. **The Indogermanic vowel-gradation.** The Indogermanic mother-language had four series of vowels, based on *e*, *ē*, *ā* and *ō*. De Saussure 134 sqq. has tried to prove, that the long base-vowels *ē*, *ā*, *ō* are contractions of *e* with a short vowel and considers the *ē*-, *ā*- and *ō*-series only as special cases of the *e*-series.

Hübschmann, Das Indogermanische vocalsystem (Strassburg 1885), Brugmann 1, 248 sqq., Bartholomae, Bezz. Beitr. 17, 91 sqq. and others assume an *a*-series and an *o*-series besides the four given above. Against this opinion Bechtel 256 sqq.

The base-vowels *e*, *ē*, *ā*, *ō* were weakened in all syllables, which had but a slight accent or no accent at all. In the latter case the radical vowel was lost without leaving any trace, but in syllables with a slight accent *e* was reduced to *ə* (Bartholomae, Bezz. Beitr. 17, 109 sqq., cf. also skr. *timirá-s* ᶜdarkᵓ: *támas* ᶜdarknessᵓ), *ē* to *e* or *ə*, *ā* to *a* or *ə*, *ō* to *o* or *ə* (Bechtel 248).

But a regular vowel-exchange is found also in accentuated

syllables: so we have an *ablaut* e : o, ē : ō, ā : ā, but the base-vowel ō is not met with in a modified form. The causes of this *ablaut* are not yet clear. Kretschmer (Kuhn's Zeitschr. 31, 366 sqq.) has shown, that G. Meyer's way of explaining it (Kuhn's Zeitschr. 24, 227 sqq.) can not be the right one.

The base-vowel e (o) often was lengthened to ē (ō): Streitberg (Idg. forschungen 3, 305 sqq.) has tried to explain this phenomenon. I see no reason to admit with Bartholomae, that there was also a *dehnstufe* of ē, ā, ō.

I. *e*-series.

	Weak:	Strong:	Lengthened:
A.	— , ə.	e, o.	ē, ō.
B.	i̯ (i), ī.	ei̯ (i̯e), oi̯ (i̯o).	ēi̯ (i̯ē), ōi̯ (i̯ō).
C.	u̯ (u), ū.	eu̯ (u̯e), ou̯ (u̯o).	ēu̯ (u̯ē), ōu̯ (u̯ō).
D.	m (m̥), əm (mə).	em (me), om (mo).	ēm (mē), ōm (mō).
E.	n (n̥), ən (nə).	en (ne), on (no).	ēn (nē), ōn (nō).
F.	r (r̥), ər (rə).	er (re), or (ro).	ēr (rē), ōr (rō).
G.	l (l̥), əl (lə).	el (le), ol (lo).	ēl (lē), ōl (lō).

When e was lost before (or after) i̯, u̯, m, n, r, l these semivowels, nasals and liquids remained consonant before vowels, but became sonant before consonants. Concerning i, ū, əm, ən, ər, əl must be observed, that they occur not only as ə-degree of ei̯, eu̯, em, en, er, el, but also as weakest degree of ei̯e, eu̯e, eme, ene, ere, ele: see de Saussure 239 sqq.; Brugmann 1, 104 sqq.; Bartholomae, Bezz. Beitr. 17, 109 sqq. I assume with Bartholomae, that i and ū are contractions of ə + i̯ and ə + u̯ and stand on a level with əm, ən, ər, əl.

II. *ē*-series.

	Weak:			Strong:	
A.	—	, ə,	e.	ē,	ō.
B.	i̯ (i),	ī,	ei̯ (i̯e).	ēi̯ (i̯ē),	ōi̯ (i̯ō).
C.	u̯ (u),	ū,	eu̯ (u̯e).	ēu̯ (u̯ē),	ōu̯ (u̯ō).

The relation of *i̯*, *u̯* to *i*, *u* in *ēi̯-* (*i̯ē-*) and *ēu̯-* (*u̯ē-*) roots is the same as in *ei̯-* (*i̯e-*) and *eu̯-* (*u̯e-*) roots: we find *i̯*, *u̯* before vowels and *i*, *u* before consonants. About the *ēi̯-* and *ēu̯-*roots see Schulze, Kuhn's Zeitschr. 27, 420 sqq.; Wiedemann, Das Litauische praeteritum (Strassburg 1891), 25 sqq. 32.

III. *ā*-series.

	Weak:			Strong:	
A.	—	, ə,	a.	ā,	ō.
B.	i̯ (i),	ī,	ai̯ (i̯a).	āi̯ (i̯ā),	ōi̯ (i̯ō).
C.	u̯ (u),	ū,	au̯ (u̯a).	āu̯ (u̯ā),	ōu̯ (u̯ō).

Concerning the roots with *i̯*, *u̯* we must observe, that the mutual relation of *i̯*, *u̯* and *i*, *u* in the weakest degree is the same as in the *e-* and *ē*-series. About the *ablaut* in *āi̯-* and *āu̯-*roots see Schulze, Kuhn's Zeitschr. 27, 420 sqq.; Kretschmer, Kuhn's Zeitschr. 31, 385 sqq.; Wiedemann 29. 32 sq.

IV. *ō*-series.

	Weak:			Strong:
A.	—	, ə,	o.	ō.
B.	i̯ (i),	ī,	oi̯.	ōi̯.
C.	u̯ (u),	ū,	ou̯.	ōu̯.

The relation of *i̯*, *u̯* to *i*, *u* in the weakest degree of roots with *i̯*, *u̯* is the same as in the *e-*, *ē-* and *ā*-series. About the *ōi̯-* and *ōu̯-*roots see Schulze, Kuhn's Zeitschr. 27, 420 sqq.;

Kretschmer, Kuhn's Zeitschr. 31, 385 sqq.; Wiedemann 29, 33 sqq.; Bechtel 274.

Examples of the vowel-gradation.

I. *e*-series.

The noun-stem *ped-*. Weak: ved. *upabdá-*, trampling, noise, avest. *frabda-*, fore part of the foot, gr. ἐπίβδαι, the day after a festival. Against our expectation we find the unweakened *e* in the gen. sing. skr. *padás*, lat. *pedis*. Strong: gr. πόδα. Lengthened: lat. *pēs*; gr. dor. πώς, goth. *fōtus*, skr. acc. sing. *pádam*, nom. sing. *pát*.

The suffix *-ter-*, for instance in *pəter-*. Weak: gen. sing. gr. πατρός, goth. *fadrs*; loc. plur. skr. *pitŕṣu*, gr. πατράσι. Strong: acc. sing. skr. *pitáram*, gr. πατέρα; gr. εὐπάτορα. Lengthened: nom. sing. skr. *pitá*, gr. πατήρ; gr. εὐπάτωρ.

Also the suffixes *-en-*, *-men-* (weak before vowels *-n-*, *-mn-*; before consonants *-n̥-*, *-m̥-*) and numerous verbal roots as *pet-*, to fly, *bheid-*, to split, *bheudh-*, to perceive, *ǵem-*, to go, *men-*, to think, *bher-*, to bear, *kel-*, to raise up.

II. *ē*-series.

The root *dhē-*, to put. Weak: 1 pers. plur. praes. ind. act. skr. *dadhmás*; part. perf. pass. skr. *-dhita-s*, *hitá-s*, lat. *crēditus*; gr. θετός, ἔθετο. Strong: 1 pers. sing. praes. ind. act. skr. *dádhāmi*, gr. τίθημι; gr. θωμός, heap, goth. *dōms*, judgment.

The root *sē-*, to throw. Weak: lat. *satus*; gr. ἐτός. Strong: gr. ἵημι, lat. *sēvi*, *sēmen*; gr. ἀφέωκα, goth. *saísō*.

III. *ā*-series.

The root *sthā-*, to stand. Weak: ved. *savyeṣṭhá* (*savyeṣṭhár-*), the warrior, who stands on the left of the charioteer; part. perf. pass. skr. *sthitá-s*, gr. στατός. Strong: 1 pers. sing. praes. ind. act. skr. *tíṣṭhāmi*, gr. ἵστημι.

The root *ăĝ-, to drive. Weak: ved. *jmán-*, path, way; 1 pers. sing. praes. ind. act. (originally *agṓ) skr. *ájāmi*, gr. ἄγω, lat. *agō*. Strong: skr. *ājíṣ*, race, contest, gr. στρατηγός, lat. *ambāges*; gr. ἀγωγή.

IV. ō-series.

The root *dō-, to give. Weak: skr. part. perf. pass. *ā-tta-s*, taken away, ved. *devá-tta-s*, given by a god; gr. δάνος, lat. *datus, dator*; gr. δοτός. Strong: 1 pers. sing. praes. ind. act. skr. *dádāmi*, gr. δίδωμι, lat. *dōnum*.

The root *ōd-, to smell. Weak: gr. ὄζω, ὀδμή, lat. *odor, oleo*. Strong: gr. ὄδωδα, εὐώδης.

Cf. Brugmann 1, 250 sqq., who differs in many points from the exposition given above.

It can not be denied, that it is very difficult to distinguish the *ē*-series from the *ā*-series, cf. skr. *cáru-*, gladsome, pleasant: lat. *cārus*, goth. *hōrs*; obg. *stēm, stām*: gr. ἵστημι (dor. ἵστᾱμι), skr. *tiṣthāmi* &c.

§ 7. **Idg. a.** The idg. *a* is represented in Aryan by *a*. Tautosyllabic *ai̯*, *au̯* were contracted in Sanskrit to *e, o*.

idg. *agṓ: skr. *ájāmi* (for *ajámi, *ajá), I drive, gr. ἄγω, lat. *agō*, icel. inf. *aka*.

idg. *aĝró-s: ved. *ájra-s*, field, plain, gr. ἀγρός, lat. *ager*, goth. *akrs*.

idg. *ak̂s-: skr. *ákṣa-s*, axle, gr. ἄξων, lat. *axis*, ohg. *ahsa*.

idg. *ak̂ró-s: skr. -*açra-*, angle (angular), gr. ἄκρος, cf. lat. *ācer* (*ák̂ro-s) and ved. *áçmā* (n), stone, gr. ἄκμων.

idg. *áṅĝhos: ved. *áṁhas*, distress, lat. *angus-* in *angustus*, cf. ved. *aṁhú-*, narrow, goth. *aggwus* and also gr. ἄγχω, lat. *angō*, gr. ἄγχι, ἀγχοῦ &c.

idg. *anə-, *ane-: skr. *ániti*, he breathes, *anilá-s*, wind, gr. ἄνεμος, lat. *animus, anima*, goth. praet. *uzōn*, expired.

idg. *anti : ved. ánti, opposite, before, gr. ἀντί, lat. ante, goth. and.

idg. *apo : skr. ápa, away, forth, off, gr. ἀπό, goth. af.

idg. *arĝ- : skr. árjuna-s, white, ved. rajatá-s, silvery, skr. rajatá-m, silver (perhaps idg. *raĝ- by the side of *arĝ-; Avestian has ĕrĕzata-, silver), gr. ἄργυρος, lat. argentum.

idg. *ĝhans- : skr. haṁsá-s, goose, swan, gr. χήν, lat. anser (*hanser), ohg. gans.

idg. *i̯aĝ- (weak form of *i̯āĝ-): skr. yájāmi (for *yajā́mi, idg. *i̯aĝṓ), I worship, gr. ἄζομαι (*i̯aĝ-i̯o-mai̯), cf. skr. yajñá-s, worship, sacrifice, gr. ἁγνός (idg. *i̯aĝnó-s), ved. yajás, worship, gr. ἄγος (idg. *i̯aĝos), ved. yajya-, venerable, gr. ἅγιος (idg. *i̯aĝi̯o-s, *i̯aĝii̯o-s).

idg. *kakud-, *kakūd- : skr. kakút (d), kakúdmān (nt), top, summit, lat. cacūmen (*cacūdmen).

idg. *kark- : skr. karká-s, karkaṭa-s, crab, gr. καρκίνος, lat. cancer (*carcer or *carcen?)

idg. *mad- : ved. mádāmi (*madā́mi), I am drunk, gr. μαδάω, lat. madeō (see Zubatý, Archiv f. Slav. phil. 13, 418 sqq.).

idg. *skandṓ : skr. skándāmi (*skandā́mi), I spring, lat. scandō.

Heterosyllabic ai̯, au̯:

idg. *sai̯ṓ- : ved. sayatvá-m, tie, from the root *sāi̯-, *sai̯-, see below.

idg. *au̯ṓ : skr. ávāmi (*avā́mi), I help, I protect, cf. lat. aveō.

Tautosyllabic ai̯, au̯, contracted to e, o:

idg. *ai̯dh- : skr. édhas, fuel, gr. αἴθω, lat. aedes, also ohg. eit, ags. ād, funeral pile.

idg. *sai̯- (weak form of *sāi̯-): skr. sétu-ṣ, joining, dam, bridge, ved. setár-, who binds, lat. saeta, bristle, ohg. seïd, ags. sāda, snare, string.

idg. *aug-: skr. *ójas*, ved. *ojmán-*, strength, power, lat. *augustus*, *augmentum*, *augeō*, goth. *aukan*, cf. gr. αὐξάνω, lat. *auxilium*.

§ 8. **Idg. ā.** Idg. *ā* = skr. *ā*:

idg. *āĝi-s*: skr. *ājí-ṣ*, race, contest, cf. gr. στρατηγός (στρα-τᾱγός) and skr. *samāja-s*, meeting, company. A weak form of the root is found in skr. *ájāmi*, gr. ἄγω, lat. *agō*, icel. inf. *aka*.

idg. *i̯āĝo-s*: skr. *-yāja-*, sacrifice (*yāga-* has got *g* by ana-logy), cf. skr. *yájāmi*, avest. *yazāmi*, gr. ἄζομαι.

idg. *bhāĝhu-s*: skr. *bāhú-ṣ*, arm, gr. πῆχυς, dor. πᾶχυς, ohg. *buog*.

idg. *bhrāter-*: skr. *bhrátā* (*r*), gr. Φράτηρ, lat. *frāter*, goth. *brōþar*.

idg. *māter-*: skr. *mātá*, gr. μήτηρ, dor. μάτηρ, lat. *māter*, ohg. *muoter*.

idg. *sthā-*: skr. *tíṣṭhāmi*, I stand, gr. ἵστημι, dor. ἵστᾱμι, lat. *stāre*.

idg. *ék̑u̯ā*: skr. *áçvā*, mare, lat. *equa*.

Heterosyllabic *āi̯*, *āu̯*:

idg. *sāi̯o-*: skr. *sāyá-m*, evening, if it belongs to *sāi̯-*, *sai̯-*, to bind, to fasten, to loosen (for the signification cf. gr. βουλῡτόνδε).

idg. *dāu̯o-*: skr. *dāvá-*, burning, fire, cf. gr. δήϊος, δέδηε. Weaker forms of this root are contained in gr. δαίω (idg. *dau̯i̯ō*), skr. *dunómi*, I burn, I torture (idg. *dunéu̯mi*).

idg. *nául̯m*: skr. acc. sing. *návam*, ship, gr. νῆα, lat. *nāvem*, cf. icel. dat. *nói*.

Tautosyllabic *āi̯*, *āu̯*:

idg. *-āi̯*: ved. dat. sing. fem. *suvapatyái*, to her who has good offspring, gr. χώρᾳ, olat. *Mātūtā*, goth. *gibai*.

idg. *$n\tilde{a}u$-s: skr. $n\tilde{a}u$-ṣ, ship, gr. ναῦς, cf. icel. *naust*.

§ 9. **Idg. e.** The idg. *e* became *a* before the separation of Indian and Iranian and fell together with the idg. *a* (see § 7) and *o* (see § 11). This change took place after the palatalization of gutturals: see § 53.

idg. *ésti*: skr. *ásti*, is, gr. ἔστι, lat. *est*, goth. *ist*.

idg. *é-bherom*: skr. *ábharam*, I bore, gr. ἔφερον.

idg. *bhérō*: skr. *bhárāmi*, I bear, gr. φέρω, lat. *ferō*, goth. *baíra*.

idg. *ĝénos*, *ĝénes-*: ved. *jánas*, family, race, gr. γένος (gen. γένεος), lat. *genus* (gen. *generis*).

idg. *ghen-*: skr. *hánmi*, I beat, I kill, gr. θείνω.

idg. *ghéros*: ved. *háras*, heat, gr. θέρος.

idg. *nébhos*: skr. *nábhas*, cloud, sky, gr. νέφος, cf. gr. νεφέλη, lat. *nebula*, ohg. *nebul*.

idg. *péñqe*: skr. *páñca*, five, gr. πέντε, lat. *quinque*, goth. *fimf*.

idg. *peq-*: skr. *pácāmi*, I cook, gr. πέσσω, lat. *coquō*.

idg. *péri*: skr. *pári*, around, gr. πέρι, goth. *faír-*.

idg. *pet-*: skr. *pátāmi*, I fly, I fall, gr. πέτομαι, πίπτω, lat. *petō*.

idg. *qe*: skr. *ca*, and, gr. τε, lat. *que*.

idg. *qeru-s*: skr. *carú-ṣ*, kettle, pot, a certain offering-porridge, icel. *hverr*.

idg. *qetuōres*: skr. *catváras*, four, goth. *fidwōr*, cf. lat. *quatuor* and gr. τέσσαρες.

idg. *réĝos*, *réĝes-*: skr. *rájas*, atmosphere, mist, gloom, dust, darkness, goth. *riqis*, cf. gr. ἔρεβος (*ereĝos*).

idg. *séĝhos*, *séĝhes-*: skr. *sáhas*, strength, might, violence, goth. *sigis*, cf. skr. *sáhāmi*, I overpower, I withstand, gr. ἔχω.

idg. *uéĝhō*: skr. *váhāmi*, I carry, gr. pamphyl. Fέχω, lat. *vehō*, goth. *-wiga*.

idg. *$u\!\!\!/qe$, *$l\!\!\!/qe$: skr. *vŕka*, voc. wolf, gr. λύκε, cf. lat. *lupe* (only for the ending of the vocative; the word *lupus* is to be separated from λύκος). Goth. *wulf* has lost the *auslaut-e.*

idg. *bhérethe*, *bhércte*: skr. *bháratha*, you bear, gr. φέρετε, goth. *baírip.*

Heterosyllabic *e͜i*, *e͜u*:

idg. *qe͜i-*: ved. *cáyate*, punishes, gr. arcad. τείω.

idg. *sme͜i-*: skr. *smáyate*, smiles, cf. gr. μειδιάω, φιλομ-μειδής, engl. *smile.*

idg. *k̂lé͜uos*: skr. *çrávas*, glory, fame, gr. κλέος.

Tautosyllabic *e͜i*, *e͜u* = skr. *e*, *o* (contracted from *a͜i*, *a͜u*):

idg. *é͜imi*: skr. *émi*, gr. εἶμι.

idg. *ĝhé͜imen-*: ved. *héman-*, winter, gr. χεῖμα, χειμών.

idg. *bhé͜udhō*: skr. *bódhāmi*, I perceive, goth. *biuda*, cf. gr. πυνθάνομαι, πεύθομαι.

idg. *ĝe͜uster-*: ved. *joṣṭár-*, *jóṣṭar-*, loving, cf. gr. γευστήριον, goblet, and skr. *juṣáte*, is glad, loves, gr. γεύω, lat. *gustus*, goth. *kiusan*, *kustus.*

§ 10. **Idg. ē̆.** The idg. *ē* became *ā* before the end of the Aryan period, but after the palatalization of gutturals (see § 53). So it fell together with the idg. *ā* (see § 8) and *ō* (see § 12).

idg. *ēd-*: skr. (Pāṇini) *áda*, have (has) eaten, *ādiván (ṁs)*, having eaten, gr. ἐδηδώς, lat. *ēdimus*, goth. *ētum.*

idg. *ēsṃ*: skr. *ásam*, I was, gr. hom. ἦα.

idg. *dhē-*: skr. *dádhāmi*, I put, gr. τίθημι.

idg. *ĝēni-*: skr. *-jāni-*, wife, goth. *qēns.*

idg. *plē-*: ved. *prātá-*, *prāṇa-*, full, gr. πλήρης, lat. *plēnus*, -plētus.*

idg. *rēĝ-*: skr. *ráj-* (nom. *ráṭ* instead of *rāk*, idg. *rēks*), king, lat. *rēx*, gall. *-rīx* (goth. *reiks* is of Celtic origin).

idg. *u̯ḗti : skr. váti, blows, gr. ἄησι (*əu̯ḗti), cf. goth. waian.

idg. *dusmenḗs : skr. durmanās, dejected, gr. δυσμενής.

idg. *si̯ḗs, *si̯ḗs : skr. syás (siyás), thou mayst be, lat. siēs, cf. gr. εἴης (*es-i̯ēs for *s-i̯ēs).

idg. *mātḗ(r) : skr. mātá, mother, gr. μήτηρ, lat. māter, ohg. muoter. The -ter- stems in Lithuanian have the nominative in -tė; so lith. motė, wife, = skr. mātá.

Heterosyllabic ēi̯, ēu̯:

idg. *u̯ēi̯u-s : skr. vāyú-ṣ, wind, air, cf. váti, gr. ἄησι.

idg. *dhēu̯ō : skr. dhávāmi, I run, cf. gr. θέω.

Tautosyllabic ēi̯, ēu̯:

idg. *é-dēi̯ksm̥ : skr. *ádāikṣam, I showed, gr. ἔδειξα.

idg. *di̯ēu̯-s : skr. dyáu-ṣ, heaven, gr. Ζεύς.

§ 11. **Idg. o.** The idg. o became a before the separation of Indian and Iranian and fell together with the idg. a (see § 7) and e (see § 9). Cf. however P. B. Beitr. 22, 546, where I have suggested a restriction of this rule.

idg. *oḱtóu̯, *oḱtó : skr. aṣṭáu, ved. aṣṭá, eight, gr. ὀκτώ, lat. octō, goth. ahtau.

· idg. *opos : ved. ápas, work, lat. opus.

idg. *osth- : skr. ásthi, bone, gr. ὀστέον, lat. os (gen. ossis from *osthes, see Zubatý, Kuhn's Zeitschr. 31, 6).

idg. *bhéronti : skr. bháranti, they bear, gr. φέρουσι, dor. φέροντι.

idg. *dedórḱe : skr. dadárça, has seen, gr. δέδορκε.

idg. *dorḱéi̯ō : skr. darçáyāmi, I let see, I show, goth. gatarhja.

idg. *dómo-s, *domu-s : ved. dáma-s, house, gr. δόμος, lat. domus.

idg. *ĝeĝóna : skr. jajána, I produced, gr. γέγονα.

idg. *g̑hono-s : skr. ghaná-s, slayer (ved.), compact, compacted mass, cloud, gr. φόνος, cf. skr. hánmi, gr. θείνω.

idg. *koksā: skr. kakṣā (kákṣa-s), region of the girth, girdle, cincture, circular wall, enclosed court, lat. coxa, mhg. hahse.

idg. *qotero-s: skr. katará-s, who (from two), gr. πότερος, ion. κότερος, cf. goth. hwapar.

idg. *moni-s: skr. maṇí-ṣ, jewel (though Vedic, this word must be a prācritism; genuine-skr. would be *mani-ṣ), os. meni, cf. lat. monile.

idg. *póti-s: skr. páti-ṣ, lord, husband, gr. πόσις, goth. -faps, cf. the feminine idg. *pótnī (gen. *potniẹ̄s or *potniẹ̄s): skr. pátnī, lady, mistress, wife, gr. πότνια.

idg. *próti: skr. práti, against, gr. προτί (πρός).

idg. *rótho-s, *rothā: skr. rátha-s, chariot, lat. rota, ohg. rad. Cf. also gr. ῥόθος, which allows however an other explication.

idg. *u̯l̥qo-s, *lúqo-s: skr: vŕ̥ka-s, wolf, gr. λύκος, goth. wulfs.

idg. *é-bhereto: skr. ábharata, gr. ἐφέρετο, 3 pers. sing. imperf. med. from the root *bher-, to bear.

Heterosyllabic oi̯, ou̯:

idg. *du̯oi̯ó-s: skr. dvayá-s, double, gr. δοιός.

idg. *óu̯i-s: skr. ávi-ṣ, sheep, gr. ὄϊς, οἷς, lat. ovis, ohg. awi.

Tautosyllabic oi̯, ou̯ = skr. e, o (contracted from ai̯, au̯):

idg. *lelói̯qa: skr. riréca, I left, gr. λέλοιπα, goth. laihw.

idg. *u̯ói̯da: skr. véda, I know, gr. οἶδα, goth. wait.

idg. *bhérois: skr. bháreṣ, thou mayst bear, gr. φέροις, goth. bairais.

idg. *bhebhóu̯dha: skr. bubódha, I perceived, cf. goth. bauþ.

idg. *sūnóu̯s: skr. sūnós, goth. sunaus, gen. of skr. sūnú-ṣ, son, goth. sunus.

I can not agree with Brugmann (Kuhn's Zeitschr. 24, 1 sqq., Morphol. unters. 3, 91 sqq.), Osthoff (Morphol. unters. 1, 207 sqq. note, cf. 4, 303 note), Streitberg (Idg. forschungen 3,

364 sqq.) and others, who suppose, that the idg. *o* in Aryan always became *ā* in open syllables. J. Schmidt (Kuhn's Zeitschr. 25, 1 sqq.) and Meillet (Mém. de la Soc. de Ling. 9, 142 sqq.) have proved, that the idg. *o* in open syllables generally is represented by *a*. The *ā* of skr. *jánu*, knee, must not be compared with the *o* of gr. γόνυ, but with the ω of gr. γωνία and skr. *dáru*, wood, is not identical with gr. δόρυ, but differs from it in the radical vowel (*ō* : *o*). So the *ā* of skr. *pádam*, *dātáram* does not correspond to the *o* of gr. πόδα, δώτορα, but to the *ō* of gr. dor. πώς, lat. *datōrem*. About the vocalisation of the causatives (skr. *svāpáyāmi* = lat. *sōpiō*) and iteratives (ved. *patáyāmi*, cf. gr. ποτέομαι) see not only Meillet, but also Delbrück, Idg. forschungen 4, 132 sq.

De Saussure 96 sq. and Bartholomae (Bezz. Beitr. 17, 93, 103) have made probable, that there was originally a difference between the *o* in the *e*-series and the *o*, which is weakened from *ō*: in Armenian *o* : *e* is represented by *o*, but *o* : *ō* has become *a*. In as early a period as the Aryan or Indo-Iranian these two *o*'s had fallen together.

§ 12. **Idg. ō.** The idg. *ō* became *ā* and fell together with the idg. *ā* (see § 8) and *ē* (see § 10). This transition took place in the same time as the change of *o* to *a*, i. e. in the Aryan period (see § 11).

idg. *ōḱú-s*: skr. *āçú-ṣ*, swift, gr. ὠκύς, cf. lat. comp. *ōcior*.

idg. *ōmó-s*: skr. *āmá-s*, raw, gr. ὠμός.

idg. *dóno-m*: skr. *dána-m*, gift, lat. *dōnum*, cf. idg. *didōti*, skr. *dádāti* (for *didāti*), gives, gr. δίδωσι.

idg. *u̯l̥qōd*: skr. *vŕ̥kād*, abl. of *vŕ̥ka-s*, wolf, cf. the Latin ablatives ending in -*ōd*, -*ō*.

idg. *bhéretōd*: ved. *bháratād*, must bear, gr. φερέτω, cf. lat. *fertō*.

idg. *su̯éso̅(r): skr. svásā (r), sister, lat. soror, goth. swistar, cf. gr. ἔορ· θυγάτηρ, ἀνεψιός.

idg. *bhéro̅: skr. bhárāmi (*bhárā), gr. φέρω, lat. ferō, goth. baíra.

Heterosyllabic o̅i̯, o̅u̯:

idg. *po̅i̯u-: ved. pāyú-ṣ, guarding, protecting, protector, gr. πῶυ. The root is *po̅i̯- (*po̅-: skr. páti, protects), *poi̯- (gr. ποιμήν), *pi- (ved. -piti-).

idg. *do̅u̯en-, *do̅men-: ved. inf. dāváne, dámane, to give. cf. gr. δοῦναι (δοϝέναι), δόμεναι.

Tautosyllabic o̅i̯, o̅u̯ (of o̅i̯ no example):

idg. *ĝóu̯-s: skr. gáu-ṣ, cow, bull, gr. βοῦς, lat. bōs (*vōs), ohg. chuo.

§ 13. **Idg. ə.** The idg. ə in general is represented in Aryan by i. So this Indo-Iranian i can be a weak form of a (idg. ė) as well as of ā (idg. ē, ā, ō). The tautosyllabic vowel-combinations əi̯, əu̯ had been contracted to i, ū before the end of the Indogermanic period.

Examples of ə : e (Bartholomae):

idg. *anə-, *ane-: skr. ánimi, I breathe, anilá-, wind: gr. ἄνεμος.

idg. *bherə-tro-m, *bhere-tro-m: ved. bharítra-m, arm: gr. φέρετρον, lat. feretrum.

idg. *ĝenə-tō̅(r), *ĝene-tō̅(r): skr. janitá̅ (r); father: gr. γενέτωρ.

idg. *isə-ró-s, *ise-ró-s: ved. iṣirá-s, strong, lively, quick: gr. ἱερός.

Further also:

idg. *təmə-ró-s: skr. timirá-s, dark: támas, darkness.

idg. *ghən-: skr. hinásmi, hiṁsāmi, I hurt: hánmi, I slay.

Other instances of idg. ə, skr. i:

idg. *pətė́(r): skr. pitá, father, gr. πατήρ, lat. pater, goth. fadar.

idg. *sthǝtó-s: skr. *sthitá-s*, standing, gr. στατός.

idg. *é-dǝto: skr. *ádita*, 3 pers. sing. aor. med. of *dádāmi*, cf. gr. ἔδοτο (idg. ǝ in δάνος).

De Saussure 150 thinks, that ǝ, when followed by $i̯$ or $u̯$, is represented in Indian by *a*, but the inaccuracy of this opinion is clearly shown by Bechtel 250 sqq. This scholar supposes, that ǝ fell together with *a*, if it had got the stress before the Aryan change of ǝ to *i*.

Instances of such *a*'s are:

skr. *rátna-m*, riches, treasure (ved.), jewel, pearl: *rātí-ṣ*, gracious, grace, gift, *rá-s* (*rāy-*), wealth, lat. *rēs*.

ved. *dátra-m*, gift: *dána-m*, *dádāmi*, gr. δῶρον, δίδωμι, lat. *dōnum*, *dōs*.

skr. *kṣatrá-m*, rule, dominion (ved.), nobility: gr. κτῆμα.

skr. *ni-dhána-m*, end, death, *dhánu-m*, prize of the contest, booty (ved.), wealth, property, money: *dádhāmi*, I put, gr. τίθημι.

Before *y*:

skr. *dáyate*, parts, allots, takes part, sympathizes, *dayá*, sympathy, compassion, gr. δαίομαι.

skr. *dháyati*, sucks, drinks: ved. *dhāyáse*, to suck, to nourish.

skr. *páyas*, sap, liquid (ved.), water, milk: *pátum*, to drink.

skr. *váyati*, weaves, *vayá*, twig (ved.): *vāna-m*, subst. weaving.

skr. *vyáyati*, envelops: *-vyāna-*, subst. enveloping.

skr. *hváyati*, calls: *hvātum*, to call.

Bechtel's theory is not improbable, but there are some objections to be made:

1° *kṣatrá-* is oxytonon: so it does not agree with Bechtel's rule.

2° in not a single of the above-mentioned words it is certain, that we have to do with idg. ǝ. If *rátna-m* really belongs

to the same root as *rātí-ṣ*, *rā́-s*, lat. *rēs*, which however seems
to be **rēi̯-*, than it might be reduced as well to **retno-m* as
to **rətno-m*, for *e* is also a weak form of *ē* (cf. θετός : τίθημι).
So *dhána-m* may be an idg. **dheno-m*, *dátra-m* an idg. **dotro-m*
(cf. δοτός : δίδωμι) &c.

In *stená-*, thief, *sénā*, army, &c. we have idg. *ai̯* (resp.
ei̯ or *oi̯*), for *əi̯* was contracted to *i* before the end of the
Indogermanic period.

The combinations ot *ə* with nasals and liquids (which existed
in Indogermanic by the side of the sonant nasals and liquids),
require a separate treatment.

In the combinations *əm*, *ən* the idg. *ə* is regularly represented by *i*:

idg. **səmó-s*: ved. *simá-s*, each, cf. *sama-s*, each, somebody
(**sm̥mó-s*).

idg. **təməró-s*: skr. *timirá-s*, dark, cf. *támas*, darkness.

idg. **bəmb-*: skr. *bímba-m*, *bímba-s*, disk, cf. gr. βέμβιξ.

idg. **g̑hən-*: skr. *hinásmi*, *hiṁsāmi*, I hurt, cf. *hánmi*,
I slay.

I assume the combinations *ər*, *əl* in those cases, where
others have supposed long sonant liquids. They remained unchanged during the Aryan period; in Iranian they became *ar*.
In Sanskrit they were treated in a different way, according
as they stood or stood not in the neighbourhood of a labial
consonant or vowel.

If they were not preceded or followed by a labial, the idg.
ər, *əl* became *ir* (*il*) before vowels, *īr* before consonants. In
the immediate neighbourhood of labials we find *ur* (*ul*) before
vowels, *ūr* before consonants.

Idg. *ər*, *əl* before vowels, not in the neighbourhood of
labials, skr. *ir*:

idg. *ǵəri-s: skr. girí-ṣ, mountain, cf. lith. giria, forest, oslav. gora, mountain.

idg. *ǵərŏ: skr. girằmi, I devour, cf. oslav. žĭrǫ, I devour, gr. βάραθρον, δέρεθρον.

idg. *gəlés: skr. girás, gen. abl. sing. of gír, voice, cf. oslav. glasŭ, voice, icel. kalla, to call (idg. *gals-) &c. There are also forms with r (lith. garsas, lat. garriō; gr. γῆρυς) and so it is possible, that the original form of girás is *gərés.

idg. *kərŏ: skr. kirằmi, I pour out, I strew.

idg. *tərŏ: ved. tirằmi, cf. idg. *térō, skr. tárāmi, I cross, and gr. τείρω, τέρετρον.

idg. *tərn̥s: ved. tirás, through, cf. lat. trans.

Idg. ər, əl before consonants, not in the neighbourhood of labials, skr. ir:

idg. *k̂ərs-: ved. çiṛṣán-, skr. çiṛṣá-m, head, cf. gr. κόρση, κόρρη and skr. çíras (idg. *k̂əros), head, gr. κάρᾱ, κάρη (*k̂ərā).

idg. *dəlghó-s: skr. dīrghá-s, long, cf. gr. δολιχός, ἐνδελεχής, lat. indulgeō.

idg. *gəl-s (perhaps *gər-s): skr. gír, voice.

Further a great number of passive participles as gīrṇá-: girằmi, kīrṇá-: kirằmi &c. It is a matter of course, that skr. jīrṇá-, worn out, old, must not be identified with lat. grānum (idg. *ĝrāno-). The ŭr of ved. jurắti, jŭryati, decays, grows frail, and other verbs, where no labial is found, is not yet explained: probably these words are loans from a dialect, where ər became ur (ūr) in every condition or they have taken their u from other verbs, in which u was developed according to the rule (sphurắti).

On the other hand we should expect ūr instead of ir in ved. irmá-s, arm, which with lat. armus, goth. arms goes back on idg. *ərmó-s (m is a labial!).

Idg. *ər*, *əl* before vowels, in the neighbourhood of labials, skr. *ur*:

idg. **u̯əren*-: ved. *úraṇa-s*, ram, lamb, cf. gr. ἀρνός, gen. of *ἀρήν.

idg. **pəlú-s*: skr. *purú-*, much, gr. πολύς (*παλύς), cf. goth. *filu*.

idg. **sphəró*: skr. *sphurā́mi*, I make a quick motion, I dart, I twitch, cf. gr. σπαίρω &c.

idg. **g̑ərú-s*: skr. *gurú-ṣ*, heavy, important, worthy of honor cf. gr. βαρύς, goth. *kaúrus* and also lat. *gravis*.

Idg. *ər*, *el* before consonants, in the neighbourhood of labials, skr. *ūr*:

idg. **u̯ərdhu̯ó-s*: skr. *ūrdhvá-s*, high, tending upwards, gr. dor. βορθό- (*ϝαρθϝό-), cf. gr. ὀρθός, lat. *arduus* (without *u̯* in the *anlaut*, idg. **ərdhu̯ó-s*).

idg. **u̯əlmí-s*: skr. *ūrmí-ṣ*, wave, ags. *wielm*, *wylm*, ohg. *walm*.

idg. **u̯əlná*: skr. *ūrṇā*, wool, cf. goth. *wulla* (but lat. *lāna* = gr. λάχνη).

idg. **pəru̯o-s*: skr. *pū́rva-s*, first, cf. oslav. *prŭvŭ* (i. e. *prĭvŭ*) and with *m* goth. *fruma*.

idg. **pəlnó-s*: skr. *pūrṇá-s*, full, cf. goth. *fulls*. Lat. *plēnus* has idg. *ē* and corresponds to ved. *prāṇa-*.

idg. **pəl-s*: skr. *pū́r*, stronghold, fortified town, cf. gr. πόλις.

idg. **məldhen*-: skr. *mūrdhā́* (*n*), head, cf. ags. *molda*.

idg. **bhərg̑o-s*: skr. *bhūrja-s* birch, cf. ohg. *pirihha*.

idg. **dəru̯ā*: skr. *dū́rvā*, millet-grass, dutch *tarwe*, wheat.

§ 14. **Idg. i.** Idg. *i* = skr. *i*.

idg. **imés*, **imén*: skr. *imás*, we go, gr. ἴμεν.

idg. **bhibhég̑mi*: skr. *bibhémi*, I am afraid, ohg. *bibēm*.

idg. **diu̯í*: skr. *diví*, in heaven, gr. Διί.

idg. **i-d*: skr. *i-d-ám*, this, lat. *id*, goth. *it-a*.

idg. *ṷidmé, *ṷidmén: skr. vidmá, we know, gr. ἴδμεν, ἴσμεν, goth. witum.

idg. *óṷi-s: skr. áviṣ, sheep, gr. ὄϊς, οἶς, lat. ovis, goth. awi-.

idg. *sṷādistho-s: skr. svádiṣṭha-s, sweetest, gr. ἥδιστος (*ᾱͩδιστος).

idg. *ésmi: skr. ásmi, I am, gr. εἰμί, lesb. ἔμμι (*ἐσμι), goth. im.

idg. *esti: skr. ásti, is, gr. ἔστι, lat. est, goth. ist.

idg. *idhi: skr. ihí (*idhí), go, gr. ἴθι.

§ 15. **Idg. ī.** Idg. ī = skr. ī.

idg. *g̑iṷó-s: skr. jívá-s, living, lat. vivus, cf. gr. βίος, goth. qius (idg. *g̑iṷo-s).

idg. *grīṷá: skr. grīvá, neck, oslav. griva, mane.

idg. *píṷen-: skr. pívā (n), fat, gr. πίων.

idg. *pī-, weakest form of *pōi̯-, to drink (not to confound with *pōi̯-, to protect): skr. pītá-s, drunk, gr. πίνω, πῖθι, cf. skr. pātum, to drink, perf. papáu, gr. πέπωκα, &c.

idg. *sīmén- (root *sī-, *sai̯-, *sāi̯-): skr. sīmá (n), crown, border, frontier, limit, cf. gr. ἱμάς.

idg. *ṷīró-s: skr. vīrá-s, man, hero, cf. lat. vir, goth. waír and gr. ἴς, ἶφι, lat. vīs. A stronger form of the root is contained in skr. váyas, strength, health, youth, age.

§ 16. **Idg. u.** Idg. u = skr. u:

Idg. *dhuǧətē(r): skr. duhitá (r), daughter, cf. gr. θυγάτηρ and goth. daúhtar, lith. dukté.

idg. *jugó-m: skr. yugá-m, yoke, generation, an age of the world, gr. ζυγόν, lat. jugum, goth. juk.

idg. *k̑unós: skr. çúnas, gr. κυνός, gen. of skr. çvá, dog, gr. κύων.

idg. *k̑lutó-s: skr. çrutá-s, heard, heard of, famed, gr. κλυτός, lat. in-clutus (cf. with ū ags. hlúd).

idg. *rudhəró-s: skr. *rudhirá-s*, red, cf. gr. ἐρυθρός (idg. *erudhró-s*), lat. *ruber*. The root *reu̯dh-, *ereu̯dh- is a secondary formation from *ereu̯, cf. skr. *aruṇá-s* and *aruṣá-s*, ruddy.

idg. *su̯ādú-s: skr. *svādú-ṣ*, sweet, gr. ἡδύς.

idg. *nu: skr. *nú*, now, gr. νύ, goth. *nu*.

I do not accept the theory, according to which idg. *ru* became *ṛ*, when there was an *u* in the following syllable: *çṛṇóti*, hears, goes back on *k̑l̥-ne-u-ti* (root *k̑elu-, cf. de Saussure 244, Pédersen, Idg. forschungen 2, 307).

§ 17. **Idg. ū.** Idg. *ū* = skr. *ū*:

idg. *bhūtí-s (root *bhū-, *bheu̯ə-, *bheu̯e-): skr. *bhūtí-ṣ*, being, prosperity, cf. gr. φύσις.

idg. *dhūmó-s: skr. *dhūmá-s*, smoke, vapor, gr. θῡμός, lat. *fūmus*.

idg. *k̑ūro-s: skr. *çūra-s*, mighty, bold, hero, gr. -κῡρος in ἄ-κῡρος, not valid, cf. τὸ κῦρος, κύριος.

idg. *mūs: ved. *mūṣ-*, mouse, gr. μῦς, lat. *mūs*, ohg. *mūs*.

idg. *nū: ved. *nú*, now, gr. νῦν.

§ 18. **Idg. m̥.** The idg. *m̥* became *a* during the Aryan period; so it fell together with *n̥* (see § 19), *a* (see § 7), *e* (see § 9) and *o* (see § 11):

idg. *gm̥skhéti: skr. *gácchati*, goes, cf. gr. imperat. βάσκε. The root is *gem-.

idg. *gm̥tó-s: skr. *gatá-s*, gone, gr. βατός, lat. *-ventus* and idg. *gm̥ti-s: skr. *gáti-ṣ*, going, issue, refuge, gr. βάσις, goth. *-qumpi-* (root *gem-).

idg. *k̑m̥tó-m: skr. *çatá-m*, hundred, gr. ἑ-κατόν, lat. *centum*, goth. *hund*. That we have to do with *m̥*, appears from lith. *szimtas*.

idg. *dek̑m̥: skr. *dáça*, gr. δέκα, lat. *decem*, goth. *taíhun*. Notice the *m* of lith. *deszimt*.

Before $i̯$, $u̯$ and before vowels we find *m̥m*:

idg. **g̑m̥mi̯ēt*: ved. *gamyā́t* must go (root **g̑em-*).

idg. **g̑eg̑m̥mu̯ós*: ved. *jaganvā́n* (*m̐s*), with *nv* from *mv* (see § 37), part. perf. act. from **g̑em-*, to go.

idg. **sm̥mó-s*: ved. *sama-s*, somebody, gr. *ἀμό-*, goth. *sums*, cf. **sэmó-s*, ved. *simá-s* each (this word has been explained differently by Geldner, Ved. studien 2, 188 sqq.).

idg. **sm̥mer-*: skr. *sámā* (*ā*-stem), half a year, year, ags. *sumor*, engl. *summer*.

§ 19. **Idg. n̥.** The dental, guttural and palatal *n̥* are represented in Aryan by *a*. They have fallen together with *m̥* (see § 18), *a* (see § 7), *e* (see § 9) and *o* (see § 11).

Instances of the dental *n̥*:

idg. **n̥-mr̥to-s*: skr. *amŕ̥ta-*, immortal, gr. *ἄμβροτος*.

idg. **mn̥tó-s*: skr. *matá-s*, thought, gr. *-ματος* in *αὐτόματος*, lat. *-mentus*, goth. *munds*.

idg. **néu̯n̥*: skr. *náva*, cf. gr. *ἐννέα*. Lat. *novem* has borrowed its *m* from *decem*, but goth. *niun* is entirely identical with skr. *náva*. Lith. *devyni* proves, that the original form had *n̥* (not *m̥*).

Before $i̯$, $u̯$ and before vowels we find *n̥n*:

idg. **mn̥ni̯etai̯*: skr. *mányate*, thinks, gr. *μαίνεται*.

idg. **g̑heg̑hn̥nu̯ós*: skr. *jaghanvā́n* (*m̐s*), part. perf. act. from **g̑hen-*, to slay.

idg. **tn̥nu̯í*: skr. *tanví*, fem. of *tanú-ṣ*, thin, cf. gr. *τανυ-*, lat. *tenuis*, obg. *dunni*.

idg. **n̥n-udro-s*: ved. *anudrá-*, waterless, gr. *ἄνυδρος*.

idg. **tn̥nú-s*: skr. *tanú-ṣ*, thin, see above.

Skr. *sánti*, they are, is not idg. **sn̥ti*, but **sénti* (Streitberg, Idg. forschungen 1, 82 sqq.).

An instance of the guttural *n̥* is:

idg. *lṇghú-s: skr. laghú-ṣ, light, swift, insignificant, gr. ἐλαχύς (*elṇghú-s), cf. ἐλαφρός (*elṇghró-s) and goth. leihts. Lat. levis seems never to have contained a nasal.

Of the palatal ṇ:

idg. *dṇk̑éti: skr. dáçati, bites, cf. gr. δάκνω, ἔδακον.

§ 20. **The problem of the long sonant nasals.** De Saussure 239 sqq., Brugmann 1, 208 sq. and others attribute long sonant nasals to the mother-language. In the same way they assume idg. ṝ, ḹ, which I have replaced by ər, əl (see § 13). These are represented in Sanskrit by ir, il (ur; īr, ūr) and stand on a level with idg. əm, ən, skr. im, in. Brugmann thinks, that those hypothetical ṃ̄, ṇ̄ became ā in Aryan. but the cases, in which such ā's are supposed, admit other explications, which seem more acceptable.

The aorist-forms skr. ágām, ágās, ágāt &c., which doubtlessly are identical with gr. ἔβην, ἔβης, ἔβη, dor. ἔβᾱν, ἔβᾱς, ἔβᾱ, are not derived from the root *g̑em-, but from its synonyme *g̑ā- (see Persson, Studien zur lehre der wurzelerweiterung und wurzelvariation, Upsala 1891, 70). The ā of skr. ágām, gr. dor. ἔβᾱν is an idg. ā (not ṃ̄) and the original paradigm was *ég̑ām, *ég̑ās, *ég̑āt &c. In a similar way are to be explained sātá-: sanómi, vātá-: vanómi, ghāta- (and ghāti-): hánmi and some other cases. But jātá-, born, seems to have taken its j instead of jñ by the influence of jánati, janáyati, jajána &c. The regular form *jñāta- (idg. *g̑n̄ātó-) corresponds to lat. -gnātus, gall. -gnātus.

The j of the praesens jáyate has the same origin as that of jātá- (tāyáte: tanóti, khāyate: khánati have been formed after the type of jáyate). The substitution of j for jñ in jātá-, jáyate is Indo-Iranian, cf. pers. zād, birth, zādan, to hear, to be born. In skr. jānámi, I know (= pers. dānam) we may explain the *j* instead of *jñ* by dissimilation (**jñānāmi*), cf. gr. *γιγνώσκω*, lat. *-gnōscō*.

If ved. *āti-ṣ*, a waterbird, is to be compared with gr. *νῆσσα*, the following explanation seems possible: there was an *-i-* (*-ei̯-, -oi̯-*) stem **nǎti-*, **ṇtéi̯-* in the mother-language, which in Aryan became regularly **nǎti-*, **atǎi̯-*. Ved. *āti-* is a contamination of **nǎti-* and **atǎi̯-*. Lat. *anas*, ohg. *anut*, lith. *antis*, oslav. *ǫty* are not clear (idg. **anat-*, **ant-*?). But perhaps it is preferable to separate *āti-* from *νῆσσα* (**nātịā*) and to identify it with gr. *ὦτίς* (*-ίδος*), as has been proposed by Speyer (Museum 2, 435).

Unexplained are ved. *áta-*, *átā*, frame of a door: lat. *anta*; ved. *yátar-*, the wife of the husband's brother: gr. *εἰνατέρες*: lat. *janitrices* &c. Von Bradke (Idg. forschungen 4, 87 sqq.) compares skr. *jārá-*, lover, paramour, with *jǎmātar-*, son in law, gr. *γαμβρός*, which combination from a semantic point of view would not seem very probable. Less credible yet is his etymology of skr. *dārá-*, wife (: gr. *δάμαρ*, 85 sqq.), for Johansson (Idg. forschungen 3, 229 sqq.) has shown its identity with gr. *δῶλος* (: *δοῦλος*).

§ 21. **Idg. ṛ, ḷ**. The idg. *ṛ* and *ḷ* are represented by *r*. Skr. *kḷptá-*, put in order, arranged, the only word that contains *ḷ*, is a prācritism for **kṛptá-* (the etymology of *kalp-* is to be found in my Etym. wörterbuch der gotischen sprache, Amsterdam 1896, s. v. *halbs*).

Idg. *ṛ* = skr. *ṛ*:

idg. **ṛkpo-s*: skr. *ṛkṣa-s*, bear, gr. *ἄρκτος*, lat. *ursus*.

idg. **ṛnéu̯mi*, **ṛnumai̯*: ved. *ṛṇómi*, I rise, I go, I attain, gr. *ὄρνῡμι* (see Schmidt, Kuhn's Zeitschr. 32, 376 sqq.), *ἄρνυμαι*.

idg. **ṛsen-*: skr. *ṛṣa-bhá-s*, bull, gr. *ἄρσην*, *ἄρρην*.

idg. *dhṛsnéu̯mi: skr. dhṛṣṇómi, I dare, cf. gr. θρασύς, θαρρέω, goth. gadaúrsan.

idg. *kṛp-: ved. kṛ́p-, appearance, form, shape, lat. corpus.

idg. mṛnámi, *mṛnamai̯: ved. mṛṇā́mi, I crush, gr. μάρναμαι.

idg. *mṛtó-s: skr. mṛtá-s, dead, ohg. mord, cf. skr. mṛtyú-ṣ, mṛti-ṣ, death, lat. mors and skr. mriyáte, dies, lat. morior.

idg. *pṛ̂kskhéti: skr. pṛcchári, asks, lat. poscit, cf. ohg. forscōn.

ldg. ḷ = skr. ṛ:

idg. *pḷthú-s: skr. pṛthú-ṣ, wide, broad, gr. πλατύς, cf. lith. platus. The original forms of the stem were *plóthu- (*plótu-) and *pḷthéu̯- (*pḷtéu̯-).

idg. *u̯ḷqo-s: skr. vṛ́ka-s, wolf, goth. wulfs, cf. idg. *lúqo-s, gr. λύκος.

idg. *ḷḱi̯o-s: skr. ṛ́çya-s, the male of an antilope, cf. ags. eolh, ohg. elaho and icel. elgr, lat. alces, russ. losǐ (also lith. elnis, oslav. jelenǐ, armen. eλn).

About skr. mriyáte, dies, kriyáte, is being made, see Brugmann 1, 113. 233. About skr. ir, īr, ur, ūr see § 13.

B. The relation of the Indian vowels to the Indogermanic.

§ 22. **The Indian vowels in general.** The Indian vocalism is distinguished from the Indogermanic by a far greater simplicity. Already in the Aryan period ə in general was changed to i and e, o, m̥, n̥ had fallen together with a, according to which ē, ō, ā were represented only by ā. Afterwards, during the separate life of Indian, ai̯ (idg. ai̯, ei̯, oi̯) and au̯ (idg. au̯, eu̯, ou̯) were contracted to e and o.

Hence it follows, that the *ā-*, *ē-* and *ō-*series had fallen together (weak: —, *i*, *a*. strong: *ā*). So there are in Indian but two vowel-series:

I. *a*-series (idg. *e*-series).

Weak:			Strong:	Lengthened:
A. —	,	*i.*	*a.*	*ā.*
B. *y* (*i*),		*ī.*	₀ (*ya*).	*āi* (*yā*).
C. *v* (*u*),		*ū.*	∪ (*va*).	*āu* (*vā*).
D. *m* (*a*,	*am*),	*im.*	*am* (*ma*).	*ām* (*mā*).
E. *n* (*a*,	*an*),	*in.*	*an* (*na*).	*ān* (*nā*).
F. *r* (*r̥*),		*ĭr* (*ŭr*).	*ar* (*ra*).	*ār* (*rā*).
G. *l* (*r̥*),		*ĭr* (*ŭr*).	*al* (*la*).	*āl* (*lā*).

II. *ā*-series (idg. *ē-*, *ā-*, *ō*-series).

Weak:	Strong:
A. — , *i*, *a.*	*ā.*
B. *y* (*i*), *ĭ*, *e* (*ya*).	*āi* (*yā*).
C. *v* (*u*), *ū*, *o* (*va*).	*āu* (*vā*).

According to the ancient Indian grammarians there was but one vowel-series. They considered *i*, *u*, *r̥* (*l̥*) as primitive vowels, which could be strengthened by a prefixed *a*-element. This strengthening was called *guṇa*. A second strengthening was produced by the further prefixion of *a* to the *guṇa*-vowel: the name of this increment was *vr̥ddhi*. It is to be noticed, that *a* is its own *guṇa*: *ā* is the corresponding *vr̥ddhi*.

So their vowel-system is as follows:

Simple vowels:	(*a*)	*i* (*ī*)	*u* (*ū*)	*r̥* (*r̥̄*).
Guṇa-vowels:	*a*	*e*	*o*	*ar.*
Vr̥ddhi-vowels:	*ā*	*āi*	*āu*	*ār.*

The older European linguists adopted this system, but the researches of the last thirty years have shown its inaccuracy (cf. § 6). It is to be observed, that the lengthened degree (*ā, āi, āu, ām, ān, ār, āl*) has extended its original dominion by the vṛddhation of vowels in secondary derivates (see von Bradke, Zeitschr. d. D. Morgenl. Ges. 40, 361 sqq.). The commencement of this secondary vṛddhation dates back to the Indogermanic period (see Bechtel 175; Streitberg, Idg. forschungen 3, 379 sqq.; also my remarks on the mutual relation of goth. *hana*: **hōn*, P. B. Beitr. 22, 189 sq., 545 sqq.).

I. *a*-series (idg. *e*-series).

idg. **pet-*, to fly, to fall.

Weak: ved. 1 pers. sing. aor. act. *ápaptam*, 3 pers. plur. perf. act. *paptúr*. Strong: skr. 1 pers. sing. praes. act. *pátāmi*, ved. 1 pers. sing. ind. iterat. act. *patáyāmi*. Lengthened: ved. 3 pers. sing. aor. pass. *ápāti*, skr. 1 pers. sing. praes. causat. act. *pātáyāmi*.

idg. **bheid-*, to split.

Weak: skr. part. perf. pass. *bhinná-s*, 3 pers. sing. praes. pass. *bhidyáte*; ved. *vibhídaka-s*, Terminalia Bellerica (the younger form *vibhítaka-* seems to be a loan from the Pāiçāci-dialect). Strong: skr. 1 pers. sing. fut. act. *bhetsyámi*, 1 pers. 3 pers. sing. perf. act. *bibhéda*. Lengthened: skr. 3 pers. sing. aor. act. *ábhāitsīt*.

idg. **bheudh-*, to perceive.

Weak: skr. part. perf. pass. *buddhá-s*, 3 pers. sing. praes. pass. *budhyáte*. Strong: skr. 1 pers. sing. praes. act. *bódhāmi*, 1 pers. 3 pers. sing. perf. act. *bubódha*. Lengthened: skr. 3 pers. sing. aor. act. **ábhāutsīt*.

idg. **gem-*, to go.

Weak: skr. 3 pers. plur. perf. act. *jagmúr*; part. perf. pass. *gatá-s*, 1 pers. sing. praes. act. *gácchāmi* (*gacchámi*), ved. 1 pers. sing. praes. act. *gámāmi* (*gamámi*). Strong: skr. 1 pers. sing. fut. act. *gamiṣyámi*, 2 pers. sing. perf. act. *jagántha*. Lengthened: skr. 1 pers. 3 pers. sing. perf. act. *jagáma*, ved. 1 pers. sing. praes. causat. act. *gāmáyāmi*.

idg. **tem-*, to be dark.

Weak: skr. *timirá-s*, dark. Strong: skr. *támas*, darkness. Lengthened: skr. *tāmrá-s*, dark-red.

idg. **men-*, to think.

Weak: ved. 2 pers. dual. perf. med. *mamnáthe*; skr. part. perf. pass. *matá-s*, 3 pers. sing. praes. med. *mányate*. Strong: skr. 3 pers. sing. fut. med. *maṁsyáte*. Lengthened: skr. 1 pers. sing. praes. causat. act. *mānáyāmi*.

idg. **bhendh-*, to bind.

Weak: skr. part. perf. pass. *baddhá-s*, 1 pers. sing. praes. act. *badhnámi*. Strong: skr. 1 pers. sing. fut. act *bandhiṣyámi*, 1 pers. 3 pers. sing. perf. act. *babándha*. Lengthened: skr. 3 pers. sing. aor. act. *ábhāntsīt*.

idg. **ter-*, to cross.

Weak: ved. part. praes. act. *títrat-*; 1 pers. sing. praes. act. *tirámi*, skr. part. perf. pass. *tīrṇá s*. Strong: skr. 1 pers. sing. praes. act. *tárāmi*, 1 pers. sing. perf. act. *tatára*. Lengthened: skr. 3 pers. sing. aor. act. *átārṣit*, 1 pers. 3 pers. sing. perf. act. *tatára*.

idg. **bher-*, to bear.

Weak: skr. 1 pers. 3 pers. sing. perf. med. *babhré*; part. perf. pass. *bhṛtá-s*; 1 pers. sing. praes. desiderat. act. *búbhūrṣāmi*. Strong: skr. 1 pers. sing. praes. act. *bhárāmi*, *bíbharmi* (*bibhármi*, Rv.), 2 pers. sing. perf. act. *babhártha*. Lengthened: ved. 3 pers. sing aor. act. *ábhārṣit*, skr. 1 pers. 3 pers. sing. perf. act. *babhára*.

II. *ā*-series (idg. *ē*-, *ā*-, *ō*-series).

idg. **dhē-*, to put.

Weak: skr. 3 pers. sing. praes. med. *dhatté*; ved. part. perf. pass. *-dhita-s*; skr. *dhána-m*, prize of the contest, booty (ved.), wealth, money. Strong: skr. 1 pers. sing. praes. act. *dádhāmi*, 1 pers. 3 pers. sing. perf. act. *dadháu*.

idg. **sthā-*, to stand.

Weak: skr. 1 pers. 3 pers. sing. perf. med. *tasthé*; part. perf. pass. *sthitá-s*. Strong: skr. 1 pers. sing. praes. act. *tíṣṭhāmi*, 1 pers. 3 pers. sing. perf. act. *tastháu*.

idg. **dō-*, to give.

Weak: skr. 3 pers. sing. praes. med. *dátte*; ved. part. perf. pass. *-dita-s*. Strong: skr. 1 pers. sing. praes. act. *dádāmi*, 1 pers. 3 pers. sing. perf. act. *dadáu*.

idg. **nāi̯-* (**nēi̯*? **nōi̯*?), to lead.

Weak: skr. 1 pers. 3 pers. sing. perf. med. *ninyé*; ved. 1 pers. plur. perf. act. *nīnimá*; skr. part. perf. pass. *nītá-s*; 1 pers. sing. praes. act. *náyāmi*, 1 pers. sing. fut. act. *neṣyámi*. Strong: skr. 1 pers. sing. praes. causat. act. *nāyáyāmi*.

idg. **dāu̯-*, to burn.

Weak: skr. 1 pers. sing. praes. act. *dunómi*; part. perf. pass. *dūná-s*; *dava-s*, fire, burning. Strong: skr. 1 pers. sing. praes. causat. act. *dāváyāmi*.

The Indogermanic mother-language had also dissyllabic roots. a great part of which contained the combinations *ei̯e*, *eu̯e*, *eme*, *ene*, *ere*, *ele*. In Indian these *udātta*-roots are found only in a weaker form, with *ayi*, *avi*, *ami*, *ani*, *ari*, *ali*, i. e. idg. *ei̯ə*, *eu̯ə*, *emə*, *enə*, *erə*, *elə*. Such roots, which make part of the idg. *e*-series, are not easily to distinguish from the idg. *ē̆*-, *ā*- and *ō*-roots. Here it will be sufficient to refer to de Saussure 239 sqq.; Brugmann 1, 104 sqq.; Kretschmer, Kuhn's

Zeitschr. 31, 386 sq.; Bartholomae, Bezz. Beitr. 17, 109 sqq.; Hirt, Idg. forschungen 7, 185 sqq.

§ 23. **Skr. a.** In skr. *a* have fallen together the idg. vowels *a, e, o, m̥, n̥.*

Skr. *a* = idg. *a*:

skr. *ájāmi*, I drive, gr. *ἄγω*, lat. *agō*, icel. inf. *aka*.

ved. *ájra-s*, field, gr. *ἀγρός*, lat. *ager*, goth. *akrs*.

skr. *skándāmi*, I spring, lat. *scandō*.

skr. *ámba*, vocat. of *ambā*, mother, cf. gr. vocatives as *νύμφα, δέσποτα*.

Skr. *a* = idg. *e*:

skr. *ásti*, is, gr. *ἔστι*, lat. *est*, goth. *ist*.

skr. *ábharam*, I bore, gr. *ἔφερον*.

ved. *jánas*, family, race, gr. *γένος*, lat. *genus*.

ved. *háras*, heat, gr. *θέρος*.

skr. *páñca*, five, gr. *πέντε*, lat. *quinque*, goth. *fimf*.

skr. *bháratha*, you bear, *ábharata*, you bore, gr. *φέρετε, ἐφέρετε*, goth. *baíriþ*.

Skr. *a* = idg. *o*:

ved. *ápas*, work, lat. *opus*.

skr. *ásthi*, bone, gr. *ὀστέον*, lat. *os*.

skr. *dadárça*, has seen, gr. *δέδορκε*.

skr. *kakṣā*, region of the girth, girdle, cincture, lat. *coxa*, mhg. *hahse*.

skr. *práti*, against, gr. *πρός*.

skr. *vṛka-s*, wolf, gr. *λύκος*, goth. *wulfs*.

Skr. *a* = idg. *m̥*.

skr. *gatá-s*, gone, gr. *βατός*, lat. *-ventus*.

skr. *çatá-m*, hundred, gr. *ἐ-κατόν*, lat. *centum*, goth. *hund*.

skr. *ratá-s*, ceased, content, gr. *ἐρατός*, cf. skr. *rámate*, stops, ceases, rests, finds pleasure in something, gr. *ἔραμαι, ἠρέμα*, goth. *rimis*.

skr. *sámā*, half a year, year, ags. *sumor*.

Skr. *a* = idg. *η*:

skr. *amŕta-s*, immortal, gr. ἄμβροτος.

skr. *matá-s*, thought, gr. -ματος, lat. -*mentus*, goth. *munds*.

ved. *anudrá-s*, waterless, gr. ἄνυδρος.

skr. *jaghána-m*, the hinder parts, the buttocks, gr. κοχώνη (*καχώνη), cf. skr. *jánghā*, lower half of the leg, and goth. *gaggan*. The first *a* in *jaghána-m* represents the idg. guttural *η*.

skr. *bahú-ṣ*, abundant, much, gr. παχύς, cf. skr. comp. *bámhiyān* (*ms*). The *a* of *bahú-ṣ* goes back on idg. palatal *η*.

Perhaps skr. *a* = idg. *ə*: see § 13.

§ 24. **Skr. ā.** By skr. *ā* are represented the idg. *ā*, *ē*, *ō*.

Skr. *ā* = idg. *ā*:

skr. *bāhú-ṣ*, arm, gr. πῆχυς, dor. πᾶχυς, ohg. *buog*.

skr. *mātá*, mother, gr. μήτηρ, dor. μᾱτηρ, lat. *mātèr*, ohg. *muoter*.

skr. *tíṣthāmi*, I stand, gr. ἵστημι, dor. ἵστᾱμι, lat. *stāre*, cf. skr. *ásthāt*, stood, gr. ἔστη, dor. ἔστᾱ.

skr. *áçvā*, mare, lat. *equa*.

Skr. *ā* = idg. *ē*:

skr. *ādiván*, having eaten, gr. ἐδηδώς.

skr. -*jāni-*, wife, goth. *qēns*.

skr. *váti*, blows, gr. ἄησι, goth. *waian*.

skr. *durmanās*, dejected, gr. δυσμενής.

Skr. *ā* = idg. *ō*:

skr. *āçú-ṣ*, swift, gr. ὠκύς, lat. comp. *ōcior*.

skr. *āmá-s*, raw, gr. ὠμός.

skr. *dána-m*, gift, lat. *dōnum*.

ved. *bháratād*, must bear, gr. Φερέτω, cf. lat. *fertō*.

§ 25. **Skr. i.** Skr. *i* goes back on idg. *i* and *ə*.

Skr. *i* = idg. *i*:

skr. *imás*, we go, gr. *ἴμεν*.

skr. *diví*, in heaven, gr. *Διί*.

skr. *ávi-ṣ*, sheep, gr. *ὄϊς, οἶς*, lat. *ovis*, goth. *awi-*.

skr. *ásti*, is, gr. *ἔστι*, lat. *est*, goth. *ist*.

Skr. *i* = idg. *ə*.

skr. *pitá*, father, gr. *πατήρ*, lat. *pater*, goth. *fadar*.

skr. *sthitá-s*, standing, gr. *στατός*.

skr. *timirá-s*, dark: *támas*, darkness, cf. also *támisrā*, darkness, dark night, lat. *tenebraė*, middle-dutch *deemster*.

skr. *girí-ṣ*, mountain, cf. lith. *giria*, forest (with idg. *r̥*) and
oslav. *gora*, mountain (with idg. *ə*, *a* or *o*).

§ 26. **Skr. ī.** In general the skr. *ī* corresponds to the idg.
ī, but before *r* + cons. it nearly always goes back on *ə*.

Skr. *ī* = idg. *ī*:

skr. *jīvá-s*, living, lat. *vivus*.

skr. *pī́vā (n)*, fat, gr. *πίων*.

skr. *sīmá (n)*, crown, border, frontier, gr. *ἱμάς (ντ)*.

Skr. *īr* before consonants = idg. *ər*, *əl*:

ved. *īrmá-s*, arm, lat. *armus*, goth. *arms*.

skr. *dīrghá-s*, long, cf. gr. *δολιχός*, *ἐνδελεχής*.

In cases as skr. *līdhá-s*, licked, *nīḍá-s*, nest, *ī* is lengthened
from *i* (see § 61 and § 63).

§ 27. **Skr. u.** In general the skr. *u* corresponds to the idg.
u, but before *r* + vowel it often represents the idg. *ə*.

Skr. *u* = idg. *u*:

skr. *urú-ṣ*, wide, cf. gr. *εὐρύς* (idg. **eu̯ru-*, **uréu-*).

skr. *yugá-m*, yoke, age, gr. *ζυγόν*, lat. *jugum*, goth. *juk*.

skr. *çrutá-s*, heard, heard of, gr. *κλυτός*.

skr. *nú*, now, gr. *νύ*, goth. *nu*.

Skr. *ur* before vowels (in the neighbourhood of labial sounds)
= idg. *ər*, *əl*:

skr. *purú-*, much, gr. πολύς (*παλύς), cf. goth. *filu*.

skr. *gurú-ṣ*, heavy, important, worthy of honor, cf. gr. βαρύς, goth. *kaúrus*.

In ved. *úraṇa-s*, ram, lamb, *ur* goes back on idg. *u̯ər*.

§ 28. **Skr. ū.** In general the skr. *ū* corresponds to the idg. *ū*, but before *r* + cons. it nearly always represents the idg. *ə*.

Skr. *ū* = idg. *ū*:

skr. *dhūmá-s*, smoke, vapor, gr. θῡμός, lat. *fūmus*.

skr. *çúra-s*, mighty, bold, hero, gr. -κῡρος in ἄκῡρος.

ved. *mūṣ-*, mouse, gr. μῦς, lat. *mūs*, ohg. *mūs*.

Skr. *ūr* before consonants (in the neighbourhood of labial sounds) = idg. *ər, əl*:

skr. *púrva-s*, first, cf. oslav. *prŭvŭ* (*prĭvŭ*) and with *m* goth. *fruma*.

skr. *púr*, fortified town, cf. gr. πόλις.

skr. *mūrdhá* (*n*), head, cf. ags. *molda*.

In skr. *ūrmí-ṣ*, wave (= ags. *wielm*, *wylm*, ohg. *walm*) and *ūrṇā*, wool (cf. goth. *wulla* with *l̥*), *ūr* represents idg. *u̯əl*; in skr. *ūrdhvá-s*, high (cf. gr. ὀρθός, lat. *arduus*), *ūr* = idg. **u̯ər*.

In cases as skr. *ūḍhá-s*, carried, ved. *dūḍáç-*, not pious, *ū* is lengthened from *u* (see § 61 and § 63).

§ 29. **Skr. e.** In skr. *e* have fallen together the idg. tauto-syllabic combinations *ai̯, ei̯, oi̯* (but in no case *əi̯*, for this diphthong was contracted to *i* before the separation of the Indogermanic dialects).

Skr. *e* = idg. *ai̯*:

skr. *édhas*, fuel, cf. gr. αἴθω, lat. *aedes*, ohg. *eit*.

skr. *sétu-ṣ*, joining, dam, bridge, cf. lat. *saeta*, bristle, ohg. *seid*, snare.

Skr. *e* = idg. *ei̯*:

skr. *émi*, I go, gr. εἶμι.

ved. *héman-*, winter, gr. χεῖμα, χειμών.

Skr. *e* = idg. *oi̯*:

skr. *véda*, I know, gr. οῖδα, goth. *wait*.

skr. *bháreṣ*, you may bear, gr. φέροις, goth. *baírais*.

Skr. *ed, edh* sometimes corresponds to idg. *ezd, ezdh* (see § 63):

ved. *sedyāt*, 3 pers. sing. optat. perf. from *sad-*, to sit, avest. *hazdyāp*.

skr. *edhí*, 2 pers. sing. imperat. from *as-*, to be.

§ 30. **Skr. o.** In skr. *o* have fallen together the idg. tauto-syllabic combinations *au̯, eu̯, ou̯* (but not *əu̯*, which was con-tracted to *ū* before the separation of the Indogermanic dialects).

Skr. *o* = idg. *au̯*:

ved. *ojmán-*, strength, power, lat. *augmentum*.

Skr. *o* = idg. *eu̯*:

skr. *bódhāmi*, I perceive, gr. πεύθομαι (πυνθάνομαι), goth. *biuda*.

ved. *joṣṭar-*, loving, cf. gr. γευστήριον.

Skr. *o* = idg. *ou̯*:

skr. *bubódha*, perceived, goth. *bauþ* (gr. *πεπουθα supplanted by πέπευθα).

skr. *sūnó-ṣ*, of the (a) son, goth. *sunaus*.

Skr. *oḍh* sometimes goes back on idg. *eg̑h* + *t* (see § 61):

skr. *vóḍhum*, to carry, cf. *váhāmi*, lat. *vehō*.

skr. *sóḍhum*, to overpower, to withstand, cf. *sáhāmi*, gr. ἔχω.

§ 31. **Skr. ṛ, ṝ, l̤, l̤̄.** Skr. *ṛ* corresponds to idg *ṛ* as well as to idg. *l̤*. The *ṝ* in some cases of the *-ar-* (*-tar-*) stems is not yet fully explained. Skr. *l̤* is found in a few forms and derivates of the root *kalp-*, but even here it is a prācritism (*kl̤ptá-s* instead of **kṛptá-s*). The *l̤̄* is not met with in any word: the Hindu grammarians added it to the alphabet only for the sake of symmetry.

Skr. *ŗ* = idg. *ŗ*:

skr. *ŕkṣa-s*, bear, gr. *ἄρκτος*, lat. *ursus*.

ved. *kŕp-*, appearance, shape, lat. *corpus*.

skr. *mŗtá-s*, dead, ohg. *mord*.

Skr. *ŗ* = idg. *ļ*:

skr. *pŗthú-ṣ*, wide, gr. *πλατύς*.

skr. *bhŕgu-ṣ* n. propr., cf. lat. *fulgur, fulgeo: flagrāre:* gr. *φλόξ, φλέγω.*

§ 32. **Skr. āi.** In skr. *āi* have fallen together the idg. tautosyllabic combinations *ą̄i̯* , *ę̄i̯* , *ǭi̯*.

Skr. *āi* = idg. *ą̄i̯*:

ved. dat. sing. fem. *suvapatyái*, to her who has good offspring, gr. *χώρᾳ*, goth. *gibai*.

Skr. *āi* = idg. *ę̄i̯*:

skr. *ádāikṣam*, I showed, gr. *ἔδειξα.*

Skr. *āi* = idg. *ǭi̯*: no example.

§ 33. **Skr. āu.** In skr. *āu* have fallen together the idg. tautosyllabic combinations *ą̄u̯*, *ę̄u̯*, *ǭu̯*.

Skr. *āu* = idg. *ą̄u̯*:

skr. *náu-ṣ*, ship, gr. *ναῦς.*

Skr. *āu* = idg. *ę̄u̯*:

skr. *dyáu-ṣ*, heaven, gr. *Ζεύς.*

Skr. *āu* = idg. *ǭu̯*:

skr. *gáu-ṣ*, cow, bull, gr. *βοῦς*, lat. *bōs* (**vōs*), ohg. *chuo*.

PART II.

SYSTEM OF CONSONANTS.

A. The representation of the Indogermanic consonants in Sanskrit.

§ 34. **The Indogermanic consonants in general.** The mother-language had semivowels, nasals, liquids, explosives and spirants.

Semivowels: i, u.

Nasals: m (labial), n (dental), $\dot{n}$ (guttural), $\tilde{n}$ (palatal). The $\dot{n}$ only is met with before velars and middle gutturals (see below), the $\tilde{n}$ before palatals, but m and n were found at the beginning of words, between vowels and in pausa. Further m occurred before labial and dental mutes, n before dental mutes.

Liquids: r, l. The existence of l in the mother-language appears not only from the fact, that the languages of Europe in general agree with each other in the distribution of r and l, but also from Fortunatov's rule (§ 44).

Explosives: To the explosives belongs the spiritis lenis, which is not indicated in writing. The other explosives were labial, dental or guttural. There were three series of gutturals,

which are not determinated with perfect physiological accuracy,
viz. the so-called velars (most backward in the mouth; they
were formed by the hindermost part of the tongue and the
soft palate), the middle gutturals (a little more in the fore-
part of the mouth; perhaps their explosion took place at
the hard palate), the palatals (most forward in the mouth;
their explosion took place at the foremost part of the hard
palate). Some scholars believe, that there were no palatal
explosives in the mother-language, and assume palatal spirants
instead of them (see Bechtel 370 sqq.): against this theory
Museum, 1, 94 sq.

So we have to assume the following series of explosives:

$$\text{Labials: } p, \ ph, \ b, \ bh.$$
$$\text{Dentals: } t, \ th, \ d, \ dh.$$
$$\text{Velars: } q, \ qh, \ \underline{g}, \ \underline{g}h.$$
$$\text{Middle gutturals: } k, \ kh, \ g, \ gh.$$
$$\text{Palatals: } \hat{k}, \ \hat{k}h, \ \hat{g}, \ \hat{g}h.$$

About *ph, th, qh, kh, k̂h* (tenues aspiratae) and *bh, dh, g̱h,
gh, ĝh* (mediae aspiratae) is to be observed, that they are
compound consonants, consisting of an explosive $+$ *h*.

Bezzenberger (Bezz. Beitr. 16, 234 sqq.) has proved, that
there was an original difference between the gutturals, which
in the western group are represented by labialized gutturals
(see § 52), and those, which in all dialects are preserved as
pure gutturals (cf. Meillet, Mém. de la Soc. de Ling. 8,
277, sqq. and Hoffmann, Bezz. Beitr. 18, 149 sqq., who do
not convince me).

As we have said above, there were also spirants in the
mother-language, viz. *s, z, j, v, þ, đ*. The existence of the
idg. *z* was discovered by Osthoff (Kuhn's Zeitschr. 23, 87 sqq.).
About *þ* and *đ* see Brugmann 1, 409 and Kretschmer, Kuhn's

Zeitschr. 31, 429 sqq. Von Fierlinger (Kuhn's Zeitschr. 27, 478 sq. note) supposes, that also in those cases, where an Indian *h* corresponds to a Greek γ, a spirant may have been the original sound: this theory however is quite uncertain and would not even seem very probable. In no case we can accept Kozlovskij's theory about an idg. χ (Arch. f. slav. phil. 11, 383 sqq.): see my remarks on this subject (Arch. f. slav. phil. 16, 380 sq.).

Semivowels.

§ 35. **Idg. i̯.** The idg. i̯ remained unchanged in Indian, except in the tautosyllabic combinations *ai̯*, *ei̯*, *oi̯*, which in Aryan fell together in *ai̯* and in Indian were contracted to *e* (see § 7, 9, 11):

idg. *i̯ó-s: skr. *yá-s*, who, gr. ὅς.

idg. *i̯ĕqr̥-t, genit. *i̯eqnós: skr. *yákr̥t* (with *a* instead of *ā* by the influence of the casus obliqui, cf. avest. *yākar̆e*), liver, gr. ἥπαρ, lat. *jecur*.

idg. *i̯aĝnó-s: skr. *yajñá-s*, sacrifice, gr. ἁγνός.

idg. *i̯udh-: skr. *yúdh-*, battle, gr. ὑσμίνη.

idg. *i̯usm-: skr. *yuṣma-*, you, gr. ῡ̔μεῖς, lesb. ὔμμες, cf. goth. *jūs*.

idg. *éi̯m(m): skr. *áyam*, I went, gr. ἤα (*ἤα).

idg. *tréi̯es: skr. *tráyas*, three, gr. τρεῖς, lat. *trēs*, goth. *þreis* (from *þrii̯iz).

idg. *médhi̯o-s: skr. *mádhya-s*, gr. μέσσος, μέσος, lat *medius*, goth. *midjis*.

idg. *gi̯ā́, *gii̯ā́: skr. *jyā́*, bowstring, lith. *gija*, thread, cf. gr. βιός, bow.

In Vedic there was an exchange of *y* and *iy* after consonants, which doubtlessly goes back to the Indogermanic period (see Brugmann 1, 112 sq. 115 sq.).

Before *ĭ* at the beginning of words *u̯* seems to have disappeared (cf. § 36).

§ 36. **Idg. u̯.** The idg. *u̯* remained unchanged in Indian, except in the tautosyllabic combinations *au̯, eu̯, ou̯*, which in Aryan fell together in *au̯* and in Indian were contracted to *o* (see § 7, 9, 11):

idg. **u̯éqos, *u̯éqes-*: skr. *vácas*, word, gr. *ἔπος*.

idg. **u̯ŏq-s*, genit. **u̯oqós*: skr. *vā́k*, voice, lat. *vōx*, gr. *ὄπ-*.

idg. **u̯óida*: skr. *véda*, I know, gr. *οῖδα*, goth. *wait*.

idg. **u̯óiko-s*: skr. *veça-s*, house, gr. *οῖκος*, cf. lat. *vīcus*, goth. *weihs* and skr. *víç-*, people.

idg. **néu̯o-s*: skr. *náva-s*, new, gr. *νέος*, lat. *novus*, cf. ved. *návya-s*, gr. *νεῖος*, lat. *Novius*, goth. *niujis*.

idg. **bhā́g̑heu̯es*: skr. *bāhávas*, arms (plur. of *bāhú-ṣ*), gr. *πήχεες, πήχεις*.

idg. **k̑u̯es-*: skr. *çvásimi*, I breathe, I sigh, lat. *queror*.

idg. **su̯ādú-s*: skr. *svādú-ṣ*, sweet, gr. *ἡδύς*, lat. *suāvis* (after the femin. idg. **su̯ādu̯í*, cf. lat. *tenuis*: skr. *tanú-ṣ*), ags. *swéte*, os. *swōti*.

idg. **sólu̯o-s*: skr. *sárva-s*, entire, all, gr. *ὅλος, οὖλος*.

In Vedic there was an exchange of *v* and *uv* after consonants, which doubtlessly goes back to the Indogermanic period (see Brugmann, 1, 140, 143).

Before *ŭ* (idg. *ŭ, ə*) at the beginning of words *u̯* was lost in Indian: examples of this rule (*úraṇa-s, ūrdhvá-s, ūrmí-ṣ, ūrṇā́*) are mentioned in § 13. Osthoff (Morphol. unters. 4, X sq. note) assumes an analogous loss of *i̯* before *ĭ* (perf. *iyā́ja*, desiderat. *íyakṣ-*: *yájati*, worships; intens. *iyasyate*: *yásyati*, gets tired with working).

In some Indian dialects *v* seems to have been changed to
m. Traces of this change are perhaps ved. *áma-s*, this: avest.
ava-, oslav. *ovŭ* and skr. *çyāmá-s*, dark; *çyāvá-s*, oslav. *sivŭ*.
But it can be hardly doubted, that sometimes there were
forms with *m* by the side of the original with *u̯* in the mother-
language. About the suffixes with *u̯*, resp. *m* see Brugmann
2, 189, 379 &c.: most striking is ved. *dámane*, gr. δόμεναι:
ved. *dāváne*, gr. δοϝέναι. Cf. also skr. *drámāmi*, I run, gr.
ἔδραμον, δέδρομα, δρόμος: skr. *drávāmi*.

Nasals.

§ 37. **Idg. m.** In general the idg. *m* remained unchanged.
Perhaps we may assume, that *mr* at the beginning of words
became *br* in Indian (skr. *bráviti*, speaks: avest. *mraoiti*, see
Osthoff, Morphol. Unters. 5, 130 sqq., but with *mr* skr. *mriyáte*:
lat. *morior* and other words).

Instances of idg. *m* = skr. *m*:

idg. **mātē(r)*: skr. *mātá*, mother, gr. μήτηρ, lat. *māter*, ohg.
muoter.

idg. **mṇtó-s*: skr. *matá-s*, thought, gr. -ματος, lat. -*mentus*,
goth. *munds*.

idg. **mṛti-s*: skr. *mṛti-ṣ*, death, lat. *mors*, genit. *mortis*.

idg. **mnā-*: skr. *mnāta-s*, mentioned, gr. μιμνήσκω, μνήσω,
μέμνημαι.

idg. **mlā-*: skr. *mlāyāmi*, I wither, gr. βλάξ, genit. βλᾶκός,
slack, lazy, stupid (**mlā-k-s*).

idg. **u̯em-*: skr. *vámāmi*, *vámimi*, I vomit, gr. ἐμέω, lat. *vomō*.

idg. **smei̯-*: skr. *smáyate*, smiles, gr. Φιλομμειδής, μειδιάω,
lat. *mirus* (skr. *vi-smayate*, is astonished), engl. *smile*.

idg. **ghormó-s*: skr. *gharmá-s*, warm, warmth, heat, lat.
formus, goth. *warms*, cf. gr. θερμός.

idg. *au̯gmen-: ved. ojmán-, strength, power, lat. augmen, augmentum.

idg. *ĝómbho-s: ved. jámbha-s, set of teeth, tooth, gr. γόμφος, ohg. chamb, engl. comb.

idg. *tó-m: skr. tám, gr. τόν, lat. is-tum, goth. þan-a, acc. pron. dem. *to-.

idg. *bhérontōm: skr. 3 pers. plur. imperat. med. bhárantām, they must bear, gr. 3 pers. plur. imperat. act. φερόντων.

Before t and u̯ the idg. m became n:

idg. *ĝémtu: ved. gántu, he must go.

idg. *ĝe ĝṃmu̯ós: ved. jaganván, having gone (cf. § 18).

The idg. combination ms is represented by n at the end of words, by m̐s between vowels:

idg. *dems: ved. dán, of the house, gr. δες- in δεσπότη: (ved. pátir dán, dámpati-ṣ).

idg. *ómso-s: skr. ám̐sa-s, shoulder, goth. ams, cf. gr. ὦμος and lat. umerus.

§ 38 **Idg. n.** In general the idg. n remained unchanged:

idg. *nā́u̯-s: skr. nā́u-ṣ, ship, gr. ναῦς, cf. lat. nāvis and icel. nó- (see Streitberg, Zur germanischen sprachgeschichte, Strassburg 1892, 49 sqq.).

idg. *nébhos: skr. nábhas, sky, gr. νέφος, cf. gr. νεφέλη, lat. nebula, ohg. nebul.

idg. *nōmṇ: skr. nā́ma (n), lat. nōmen, cf. gr. ὄνομα and goth. namō.

idg. *séno-s: ved. sána-s, old, gr. fem. ἕνη, cf. lat. senex and goth. sincigs.

idg. *u̯idmenai̯: ved. vidmáne, to know, gr. ἴδμεναι.

idg. *su̯épno-s, *supnó-s: skr. svápna-s, sleep, lat. somnus, icel. svefn, with idg. u gr. ὕπνο:.

idg. *bhéndhono-m: skr. bándhana-m binding, band, bond,

goth. *bindan*, cf. skr. *bándhu-ṣ*, connection, relative, friend, gr. πενθερός, father in law, and lat. *offendix*, *offendimentum*.

idg. **tékpon*: skr. voc. *tákṣan*, carpenter, gr. τέκτον·

After *c* and *j* (idg. *q̇*, *k̇*, resp. *g̣*, *g*, *ĝ*) *n* was palatalized: so idg. **i̯aĝnó-s* became skr. *yajñá-s*, sacrifice. The only instance of *ñ* (idg. *n*) after *c* is skr. *yācñá*, request: *yácate*, asks.

After *ṣ*, *r*, *ṛ*, *ṝ* the dental nasal was turned into the lingual *ṇ*:

idg. **kṛsno-s* (**qṛsno-s?*): skr. *kṛṣṇá-s*, black, opruss. *kirsna-*, cf. oslav. *črĭnŭ*.

idg. **usnó-s*: skr. *uṣṇá-s*, hot: ὄσαμι, I burn, gr. εὕω, lat. *ūrō*. Cf. lith. *usnis*, thistle.

idg. **érnos*: ved. *árṇas*, flood, stream, cf. ohg. *ernust*, ags. *eornost* (see my Etym. wb. der got. sprache s. v. *arniba*).

idg. **mṛnámi*: ved. *mṛṇámi*, I crush, gr. med. μάρναμαι.

idg. **tṛno-m*: skr. *tṛ́ṇa-m*, grass, cf. goth. *paúrnus*.

Not only if *ṣ*, *r*, *ṛ*, *ṝ* immediately preceded, the dental *n* was lingualized: the change of *n* to *ṇ* took place, at whatever distance from it the lingual consonant or vowel might be found, unless there intervened a palatal affricate, a *ç*, a dental or a lingual (see Whitney § 189 sqq.). Instances:

skr. *dvéṣāṇi*, 1 pers. sing. praes. conj. (imperat.) of *dvéṣmi*, I hate.

ved. *cákṣaṇa-m*, sight, appearance: *cáṣṭe*, appears, sees, looks.

skr. *Rudréṇa*, instr. sing. of *Rudrá-s*.

skr. *váriṇe*, dat. sing. of *vári*, water.

skr. *kriṇámi*, I buy, cf. gr. ἐπριάμην.

skr. *cíkīrṣamāṇa-s*, part. praes. of *cíkīrṣate*, desires to do (desid. of *karóti*, does).

The idg. combination *ns* is represented by *n* at the end of words (cf. Lorentz, Bezz. Beitr. 21, 173 sqq.), by *ṁs* between vowels:

4

idg. *u̯ĺqons: skr. acc. plur. *vŕkān*, wolves, cf. gr. λύκους, lat. *equōs*, *lupōs*, goth. *wulfans*, *dagans* (also skr. acc. plur. *agnín*, *paraçún*, cf. goth. *anstins*, *sununs* &c.).

idg. *ĝhans-: skr. *haṁsá-s*, goose, swan, gr. χήν, ohg. *gans*, cf. lat. *anser*.

About idg. *ln (rn)*, skr. *ṇ* see § 44.

§ 39. **Idg. ṅ.** The idg. *ṅ* remained unchanged, unless the following guttural (resp. velar) was palatalized by the influence of a palatal vowel:

idg. *oṅko-s: skr. ˙aṅká-s, lap, hook, gr. ὄγκος, lat. *uncus*, cf. goth. *hals-agga*.

idg. *bhoṅgo-s, *bhoṅgā: skr. *bhaṅgá-s*, wave, lith. *banga*.

But *ṅ* became *ñ*, if the following guttural (resp. velar) was changed into a palatal affricate:

idg. *péṅqe: skr. *páñca*, five, gr. πέντε, lat. *quinque*, goth. *fimf*.

§ 40. **Idg. ñ.** The idg. *ñ* remained unchanged before idg. *ĝ*, skr. *j*, but it became *ṁ* before idg. *k̑*, skr. *ç* and before idg. *ĝh*, skr. *h*. In other words: if the following palatal guttural became a spirant, *ñ* was reduced to anusvāra.

idg. *ēnóñka: skr. *ānáṁça*, I attained (perf. of *açnómi*, idg. *ṇk̑néu̯mi*), cf. *áṁça-*, portion, part, gr. ἤνεγκον, ἐνήνοχα, lat. *nanciscor*.

idg. *áñĝhos: ved. *áṁhas*, distress, lat. *angus-* in *angustus*, cf. gr. ἄγχω, lat. *angō* &c.

Liquids.

§ 41. **The liquids in general.** Nowadays no one doubts any more, but that the mother-language, possessed at least two liquids, viz. *r* and *l*. Since the clever article of Fortunatov on the representation of dental + liquid in Indian, it

may be called very probable, that the ancient difference between
r and *l* still existed in the Aryan period. In Iranian *r* and *l*
fell together into *r* and in the Vedic dialect of Indian *l* is
but rare: in most cases epic and class. *l* is represented by
ved. *r*. Therefore we need not be surprised, that the older
linguists considered *l* as younger than *r*.

Yet it can not be denied, that in as early a period
as the Indogermanic there often stood forms with *r* and
l side by side with each other (*l* : *r* in suffixes see Brugmann 2, § 62, 74—77, 98, 107, 119—122; in root-sylla-
bles Persson, Studien zur lehre v. d. wurzelerweiterung &c.,
Upsala 1891, 59—67, cf. P. B. Beitr. 17, 437 sqq. and
my Etym. wb. der got. sprache s. v. *alhs, baírhts, biraubōn,
gras, grēdus, hrūk, kalbō, stilan*). This Indogermanic change of
r and *l* does not properly belong to the province of Indian
phonetics and so we may leave it unnoticed. Likewise such
cases as skr. *bhunákti* : goth. *brūkjan*, skr. *bhanákti* : goth.
brikan are to be explained by phonetic rules of the mother-
language.

§ 42. **Idg. r.** In general the idg. *r* remained unchanged.
Instances are:

idg. **régi̯ō* : skr. *rájyāmi*, I am (get) red, affected with a
strong feeling, gr. ῥέζω.

idg. **rē-s* : skr. *rá-s*, wealth, lat. *rēs*.

idg. **rēk̂-s*, stem **rēĝ-* : skr. *rát̲* (instead of **rāk* from **rākṣ*,
which was to be expected), lat. *rēx*.

idg. **reu̯d-* : skr. *ródimi*, I weep, lat. *rūdō*, ags. *réotan*.

idg. **bhérō* : skr. *bhárāmi*, I bear, gr. φέρω, lat. *ferō*, goth.
baíra.

idg. **péri* : skr. *pári,* around, gr. πέρι, lat. *per*, goth. *faír-*.

idg. **smérō* : skr. *smárāmi*, I remember, cf. lat. *memor*.

idg. *dedórka: skr. dadárça, I saw, gr. δέδορκα.

idg. *ger-: skr. jāgármi, I wake, gr. ἐγείρω, ἐγρήγορα.

idg. *grasô: skr. grásāmi, I eat, I devour, gr. γράω.

idg. *qrināmi: skr. krīṇ́ami, I buy, cf. gr. ἐπριάμην.

idg. *máter: skr. vocat. mátar, mother, gr. μῆτερ.

About the combinations of r with dentals see § 44. Un-explained is the l in cases as skr. luñcāmi, I pull out, I pull off, I husk: gr. ὀρύσσω, lat. runcāre; skr. lumpámi, I break (already ved., by the side of rúpyāmi, I have belly-ache): lat. rumpō, ags. réofan, and many others. In some of them we must assume an Indogermanic change of r and l.

§ 43. **Idg. l.** In Vedic the idg. l has fallen together with r, except when followed by a dental. The words, containing l are to be considered as loans from an other dialect. In the epic and classical language the original l is represented in some cases by l, in other cases by r; often the same word occurs in two forms, with l and with r. The distribution of the two liquids in the Brāhmaṇa's is nearly the same as in classical Sanskrit. I am inclined to believe, that the idg. l regularly remained unchanged in Sanskrit: the forms with r may have been borrowed from other dialects. Hence it appears, that the Sanskrit of Madhyadeça is not a younger form of the western dialect, in which the hymns of the Ṛgveda have come down to us.

Idg. l = skr. l:

idg. *lambetai: skr. lámbate, hangs down (already Çat. Br., but Rgv. rámbate), cf. lat. lābor.

idg. *lẹ̆ghmi: skr. léhmi, I lick (but ved. réhmi), cf. gr. λείχω, lat. lingō and goth. -laigōn.

idg. *limpô: skr. limpámi, I smear (already Athv. and Brāhm., but Rgv. rip — except however 1, 191, 1-4 alipsata), cf.

gr. λίπος, λιπαρός, ἀλείφω, ἀλοιφή, lat. *lippus*, goth. *bi-leiban*, *laiba*, *liban*.

idg. **lubh-*, **leubh-*: skr. *lúbhyāmi*, I desire (already Athv. and Brāhm., even Rgv. 10, 103, 12 *lobháyanti*), lat. *lubet*, goth. *liufs*.

idg. **təlá*: skr. *tulá*, balance (already Vājasaneyi-saṃhitā and Brāhm.; with unexplained *u* instead of *i*), cf. gr. τάλαντον, τελαμών, lat. *tollō*, goth. *þulan*.

idg. **aĺpo-s* (**oĺpo-s*?): skr. *álpa-s*, small, cf. lith. *alpti*, to languish, to swoon away, *alpnas*, weak, fainted (also gr. ἀλαπαδνός?).

ldg. *l* = skr. *r*:

idg. **lékṣō*, **əlékṣō*: skr. *rákṣāmi*, I guard, I protect, gr. ἀλέξω.

idg. **lelóiqa*: skr. *riréca*, I left, gr. λέλοιπα, goth. *laihw*, perf. of skr. *riṇácmi*, gr. λείπω, goth. *leihwa*.

idg. **léudhō*: skr. *róhāmi* (ved. also *ródhāmi*, which is the older form), I rise, I grow, goth. *liuda*, cf. gr. ἐλεύσομαι, εἰλήλουθα.

idg. **pel-*, **plē-*: skr. *píparmi*, I fill, gr. πίμπλημι, πληρής, lat. *im-pleō*, *plēnus*, cf. with *ḷ* goth. *fulls*.

idg. **pléthetai*: skr. *práthate*, broadens, cf. *pṛthú-ṣ*, broad, gr. πλατύς.

About the combinations of *l* with dentals see § 44.

§ 44. **Combinations of r and l with dentals.** Fortunatov (Bezz. Beitr. 6, 215 sqq.) has given the following rule: *r* + dental remained unchanged, but in the combinations of *l* and a following dental the *l* disappeared and the dental was lingualized. It is to be noticed, that the word *dental* is taken here in its widest sense. Bechtel 382 sqq., Windisch (Kuhn's Zeitschr. 27, 168), Darbishire (Relliquiae philologicae, Cambridge 1895, 202 sqq. 241 sqq.) and many other scholars have accepted this rule, but Brugmann 1, 213, Bartholomae (Idg. forschungen 3, 157 sqq.), J. Schmidt (Kritik der sonantentheorie 1 sq. note) and Wackernagel 1, 171 prefer to believe, that all those linguals, which go back on a combination of liquid + dental are due to Prācritic influence.

Examples of *r* + dental:

idg. **kértō*: skr. *kártāmi* (epic, the classical praesens is *kṛntāmi*), I cut, lith. *kertu*.

idg. **u̯értō*: skr. *vártāmi* (more common med. *várte*), I turn, move, go on, abide, exist, am, am present, lat. *vertō*, goth. *waírþa*.

idg. **mérdō*: skr. *márdāmi*, I press, squeeze, crush, destroy, cf. lat. *mordeō* (= skr. causat. *mardáyāmi*).

idg. **pérdetai̯*: skr. *párdate* (Dhātup.), breaks wind, gr. πέρδεται, cf. hg. *firzen, furzen*.

idg. **ardho-s* (**ordho-s?*): skr. *ardhá-s*, half, cf. lith. *ardýti*, to separate.

idg. **ghordho-s*: skr. *gardha-s*, desire, avidity, cf. goth. *grēdus*, hunger.

idg. **kórno-s*: skr. *kárṇa-s*, ear.

idg. **u̯órno-s*: skr. *várṇa-s*, cover, outside, color, caste, sound, akin to *vṛṇómi*, I cover, *várūtha-m*, cover, protection, gr. ἔρυσθαι, goth. *warjan* &c.

idg. **dhérsō*: skr. *dhárṣāmi* (more common *dhṛṣṇómi*), I dare, cf. gr. θαρσέω, θαρρέω, θαρσαλεός, θρασύς &c., goth. *ga-dars*.

idg. **u̯ersā*: skr. *varṣá*, rain, gr. ἔρση, ἔρση, ἐέρση.

Examples of *l* + dental:

idg. **palto-s*: skr. *paṭa-s*, woven stuff, cloth, garment, cf. oslav. *platǐno*, russ. *polotnó*, linen, perhaps also skr. *paṭála-m,* cover, veil, mass, gr. (thrac.?) πέλτη, a little shield, and icel. *feldr*, cover.

idg. **paltu-s*: skr. *paṭu-ṣ*, sharp, cf. gr. πλατύς, saltish, brack.

idg. **sphalt-*: skr. *spháṭāmi*, I burst (Dhātup. *visaraṇe*), ohg. *spaltan* (from *spaldan* with germ. *d* from *þ* by Verner's law).

idg. **u̯alto-s*: skr. *vaṭa-s* (*vaṭa-m*, *vaṭi*), snare, cf. lith. *valtis*, thread, net, russ. *vólotĭ*, thread.

idg. **ghŏlto-*: skr. *hāṭaka-m*, gold (also „Goldland", a certain country in India, the inhabitants of which were called *Hāṭakās*), oslav. *zlato*, russ. *zóloto*, cf. with *l̥* goth. *gulþ*.

idg. **gelth-* (**ĝelth-*?): skr. *jaṭhára-m*, belly, womb, goth. *kilþei* (cf. with *r* skr. *jartú-*, vulva, Uṇādisūtra).

idg. **kulth-*: skr. *kuṭhāra-*, axe, lat. *culter*.

idg. **kəlno-s*: skr. *kiṇa-s*, callosity, lat. *callus* (*callum*).

idg. **kulni-s*, **kulno-s*: skr. *kuṇi-ṣ*, lame of one arm, gr. κυλλός.

idg. **ŏlní-s*: skr. *āṇí-ṣ* (*aṇi-ṣ*), the leg immediately above the knee, linch-pin, cf. gr. ὠλένη, lat. *ulna*, goth. *aleina* and ohg. *lun*, os. *lunisa*, ags. *lynes*, linch-pin (with *lu* from *l̥*?).

idg. **pălní-s*: skr. *pāṇí-ṣ*, hand, cf. gr. παλάμη, lat. *palma* and ags. *folm*.

idg. **pélno-s*: skr. *paṇa-s*, wager, stake, prize, wages, a coin &c., lith. *pelnas*, wages, oslav. *plĕnŭ*, booty, cf. gr. πωλέω and ohg. *fāli*.

idg. **u̯ălnī*: ved. *váṇi*, reed, rush, cf. goth. *walus*.

idg. **bhăls-*: skr. *bháṣate*, speaks, *bháṣati*, barks, lith. *balsas*, voice, tone, icel. *bjalla*, engl. *bell*.

idg. **lals-*: skr. *láṣāmi*, I desire, cf. *lālasa-s*, desirous, gr. λιλαίομαι and goth. *lustus* (*lu* from *l̥*?).

idg. **pĕls-*: skr. *pāṣāṇá-s*, ved. *pāṣyà-*, stone, gr. πέλλα· λίθος, cf. ohg. *felis*.

The apparent exceptions to Fortunatov's rule may be explained as prācritisms. Such cases are:

skr. *bhaṭa-s*, soldier: *bhṛtá-s*, hired (cf. gr. φέρω).

skr. *káṭa-s*, mat: *kartana-m*, spinning (cf. gr. κύρτος).

skr. *kaṭú-ṣ*, sharp: **kartú-ṣ* (cf. lith. *kartus*).

skr. *naṭa-s*, dancer, actor: *nartaka-s*, dancer (*nṛtyāmi*, I dance).

By no means all linguals go back on *l* (*r*) + dental, but they are often original dentals, which are lingualized by Prācritic influence. Instances are skr. *aṭāmi*, I roam, I wander about: ved. *átāmi*; skr. *bhaṇāmi*, I speak: ved. *bhánāmi* &c.

§ 45. **Metathesis of r.** On this subject see Brugmann 1, 214 and Persson, Studien zur lehre v. d. wurzelerweiterung 218 sqq. Instances of *ra : ar*: fut. *drakṣyámi*, perf. 2 pers. sing. *dadráṣṭha*, inf. *dráṣṭum* from the root *darç-*, idg. **derk̂-*, to see; perf. 2 pers. sing. *tatráptha* (*tatárptha*) from the root *tarp-*, idg. **terp-*, to be satisfied; fut. *srapsyámi* (*sarpsyámi*), aor. *ásrāpsam* (*ásārpsam*) from the root *sarp-*, idg. **serp-*, to creep.

Labial explosives.

§ 46. **Idg. p.** Idg. *p* = skr. *p*:

idg. **pətḗ(r)*: skr. *pitá*, gr. πατήρ, lat. *pater*, goth. *fadar*.

idg. **pərós*: skr. *purás*, in front, forward, before, gr. πάρος, cf. goth. *faúra*.

idg. **pelek̂u-s*: skr. *paraçú-ṣ*, axe, gr. πέλεκυς, cf. goth. *filhan, filigri*.

idg. **pṛk̂ni-s*: skr. *pṛçni-ṣ*, speckled, cf. gr. περκνός and perhaps ohg. *forhana*, trout.

idg. **perut*: skr. *parut*, last year, cf. gr. πέρυσι, dor. πέρυτι, mhg. *vert*.

idg. *pró: skr. prá-, forward, onward, gr. πρό, goth. fra-, cf. lat. pród, pró.

idg. *pléu̯ō: skr. plávāmi, I float, I swim &c., gr. πλέω, cf. lat. pluit and with suffix -d ags. fléotan.

idg. *népōt-s: ved. nápāt, descendant, grandson, lat. nepōs, ohg. nefo.

idg. *su̯épno-s: skr. svápna-s, sleep, dream, lat. somnus, icel. svefn, cf. gr. ὕπνος.

idg. *sérpō: skr. sárpāmi, I creep &c., gr. ἕρπω, lat. serpō.

idg. *spéḱ-s: ved. spáṭ (instead of *spak, stem spaç-), lat. -spex in auspex, haruspex, cf. skr. páçyāmi (Dhātup. also spáçāmi), lat. specio, ohg. spehōn.

How far the Aryan ph (skr. ph, iran. f) goes back on idg. ph, is still unsettled (cf. Hoffmann, Bezz. Beitr. 18, 154 sqq.). Instances of skr. ph, iran. f:

skr. kapha-, phlegm, avest. kafa-.

skr. çaphá-, hoof, avest. safa-.

§ 47. **Idg. b.** Idg. b = skr. b (cf. P. B. Beitr. 18, 236 sqq. 20, 325 sqq.):

idg. *bolo-m: skr. bála-m, strength, power, cf. oslav. bolij, greater, larger, lat. dē-bilis, powerless, weak (cf. von Grienberger, Zeitschr. für deutsche philologie 27, 453 sqq. and Osthoff, Idg. forschungen 6, 1 sqq.).

idg. *bālo-s (ā or ō?): skr. bālá-s, young, foolish, white-russ. bal, liar, cf. also russ. balováti, to dally, to fondle, to spoil.

idg. *balbal-, *barbar-: skr. balbalā-karomi, I stammer, barbará-s, stammering, gr. βάρβαρος, cf. lat. balbus with broken reduplication.

idg. *bal-: ved. balbalīti, whirls (Uccāir dhūmaḥ paramayā jūtyā balbalīti, Çat. Br.), cf. gr. βαλλίζω.

idg. *buk-: skr. buk-kāra-s, roar, bellow, gr. βύκτης, βυκάνη, lat. būcina.

idg. *belk-, *blek-: skr. bárkara-s, kid, slov. blekati, to bleat, blekaš, bleating buck.

idg. *buli-s: skr. buli-ṣ, cunnus, buttock, lith. bulis, buttock, cf. lat. bulla, bubble, lith. bumbulas, knob, knot, bumbulys, turnip, russ. búlka, roll (bread), dutch peul, husk, pulse, puilen, to swell (in speaking of eyes: to start from the head).

idg. *bāl- (with ā or ō?): skr. jam-bāla-s, pool, mud (jam-, earth, + -bāla-s), ags. pól, swed. pöl, cf. lith. bala and oslav. blato, russ. bolóto.

idg. *pibō: skr. píbāmi, I drink, lat. bibō (irish ebaim proves, that the first consonant was an idg. p).

idg. *lamb-, *lāb-: skr. lámbate, hangs down, lat. lābitur, cf. goth. slēpan, ags. slǽpan, to sleep, ohg. slaf, dutch slap, slack, oslav. slabŭ, weak.

idg. *-bd-: ved. upa-bdá-s, stamping, trampling, gr. ἐπίβδαι, the day after a feast, cf. πεδά, immediately after, and skr. pát, foot, gr. πούς &c.

§ 48. **Idg. bh.** Idg. bh = skr. bh:

idg. *bhérō: skr. bhárāmi (bíbharmi), I bear, gr. φέρω, lat. ferō, goth. baíra.

idg. *bhéu̯ō: skr. bhávāmi, I am, cf. gr. φύω, lat. fui, ohg. būan.

idg. *bhrátē(r): skr. bhrátā, gr. φράτηρ, lat. frāter &c.

idg. *bhrū-s, *əbhrū-s: skr. bhrú-ṣ, eye-brow, gr. ὀφρῦς (from *ἀφρῦς, cf. Schmidt, Kuhn's Zeitschr. 32, 376 sqq.), cf. oslav. brŭvĭ, obrŭvĭ and ohg. brāwa.

idg. *nébhos: skr. nábhas, cloud, sky, gr. νέφος, cf. gr. νεφέλη, lat. nebula, ohg. nebul.

idg. *ǵómbho-s: skr. jámbha-s, set of teeth, tooth, gr. γόμφος, ohg. chamb.

When followed by an aspirate, *bh* lost its aspiration:

idg. **bhéųdhō*: skr. *bódhāmi*, I perceive, goth. *biuda*, cf. gr. πυνθάνομαι, πεύθομαι.

idg. **bhņdhnámi*: skr. *badhnámi*, I bind, cf. *bándhana-m*, binding, band, bond, goth. *bindan*: to this root belong also skr. *bándhu-ş*, connection, relative, friend, gr. πενθερός and lat. *offendimentum*, *offendix*.

Idg. *bh* + *t* is represented by *bdh*: see § 49.

We must assume with von Bradke (Zeitschr. der D. Morgenl. Ges. 40, 657 sqq.), that the not very numerous cases, in which the idg. *bh* is represented by skr. *h*, are loans from a Prācritic dialect. So we find skr. *gṛhņámi*: ved. *gṛbhņámi*, I seize; skr. *hárāmi*, I bear, I take: *bhárāmi*, I bear. Cf. prākr. *pahu-*: skr. *prabhú-*, lord; prākr. *hodi*, *hoï*: skr. *bhávati*, is, &c.

Dental explosives.

§ 49. **Idg. t.** Idg. *t* = skr. *t*:

idg. **tņnéųmi*: skr. *tanómi*, I stretch, cf. gr. τείνω, lat. *tendō*, *tentus*, goth. *-þanjan*. To the same root skr. *tanú-ş*, thin, gr. τανυ-, lat. *tenuis*, ohg. *dunni*.

idg. **tudó*: skr. *tudámi*, I push, I strike, cf. ved. *tundate*, *tundāná-*, lat. *tundō* and goth. *stautan*.

idg. **tréįes*: skr. *tráyas*, three, gr. τρεῖς, lat. *trēs*, goth. *þreis*.

idg. **pétō*: skr. *pátāmi*, I fly, I fall, lat. *petō*, cf. gr. πέτομαι, πίπτω.

idg. **ųértetaį*: skr. *vártate*, turns, rolls, goes, abides, cf. lat. *vertō*, goth. *waírþa*.

Idg. *tn* remained unchanged in Indian:

idg. **pótnī*: skr. *pátnī*, lady, mistress, wife, cf. gr. πότνια.

idg. **rətnó-m* (**retno-m*?): skr. *rátna-m* (by the side of *ratná-m*), riches, treasure (ved.), jewel, pearl, cf. § 13.

After *ṣ* the dental *t* was lingualized:

idg. **oḱtŏ(u̯)*: skr. *aṣṭá* (ved.), *aṣṭáu*, eight, gr. ὀκτώ, lat. *octō*, goth. *ahtau*.

idg. **ustó-s*: skr. *uṣṭá-s*, burned, lat. *ustus*.

Before *c* the dental *t* was palatalized:

idg. **utko-*, **utke-*: skr. *ucca-* (from **utca-*), high, derived from idg. **ŭd*, skr. *úd*, up, forth, out, goth. *ūt*, ags. *út*.

Akin to the assimilation of *tc* to *cc* was the transition of *tç* to *cch*: so *pacchás*, in hemistichs, goes back on **pat-çás*, **pad-çás*, derived from *pad-*, *pād-*, foot, quarter of a stanza.

The idg. combination *lt* became *ṭ*, see § 44.

Very difficult are the combinations of mediae aspiratae with *t*, which seem to be changed to mediae + *dh* before the end of the Indogermanic period.

Idg. *bh* + *t* = skr. *bdh*:

ved. *dabdhá-s*, harmed, hurted, deceived: *dabhnómi*.

skr. *labdhá-s*, seized, taken, got: *lábhe*.

Idg. *dh* + *t* = skr. *ddh*:

skr. *baddhá-s*, bound: *badhnámi*.

skr. *buddhá-s*, perceived, awake: *bódhāmi*.

Idg. *g̑h* + *t* and *gh* + *t* = skr. *gdh*:

skr. *dagdhá-s*, burned: *dáhāmi*.

Idg. *ĝh* + *t* = skr. *ḍh*:

ved. *sāḍhá-s*, conquered: *sáhāmi*.

skr. *ūḍhá-s*, carried: *váhāmi*.

How far the Aryan *th* (skr. *th*, iran. *þ*) represents an idg. *th*, is not sufficiently clear. A certain case of idg. *th* is the suffix of the 2 pers. sing. perf. *-tha*:

idg. **u̯óittha*: skr. *véttha*, thou knowest, gr. οἶσθα, cf. goth. *waist* and see Zubatý, Kuhn's Zeitschr. 31, 4.

Instances of skr. *th*, iran. *þ*:

skr. *rátha-*, chariot, avest. *rapa-*.

skr. *pṛthú-*, wide, avest. *pĕrĕpu-*.

§ 50. **Idg. d.** Idg. *d* = skr. *d*:

idg. **didōmi*: skr. *dádāmi*, I give (**didāmi*), gr. δίδωμι, cf. lat. *dō*.

idg. **dékm̥*: skr. *dáça*, ten, gr. δέκα, lat. *decem*, goth. *taíhun*.

idg. **dru-*: ved. *dru-*, wood, gr. δρυτόμος, δρῦς, cf. goth. *triu* (idg. **dreu̯-*), gr. δόρυ (idg. **dóru*), skr. *dáru* (idg. **dŏru*).

idg. **du̯ŏ(u̯)*: ved. *dvá*, skr. *dváu*, two, gr. δύω, lat. *duō*, cf. goth. *twai*.

idg. **sédos*: skr. *sádas*, seat, gr. ἕδος: skr. root *sad-*, to sit, lat. *sedeō*, goth. *sitan* &c.

idg. **skhind-*: skr. *chindánti*, they cut off, gr. σχινδαλμός, splinter, lat. *scindō* (cf. goth. *skaidan*, idg. root **skhai̯t-*).

During or more likely long before the Aryan period *dd*, *ddh* were changed to *zd*, *zdh*. In Iranian the *z* of these combinations was preserved, but in Indian it disappeared after having developed an *i*. Example:

idg. **deddhí* (or already **dezdhí*): ar. **dazdhi*, avest. *dazdi*, skr. *dehí* (instead of **dedhí* from **daidhi*, **daizdhí*), give.

In certain cases *zd* became *ẓd* in Aryan, from which skr. *ḍ* (see § 63):

idg. **nizdó-s*: skr. *niḍá-s*, nest, lat. *nīdus*, ohg. *nest*.

About the lingualization of *d* in *ld* see § 44.

Idg. *dn* was assimilated in Indian to *nn* (cf. however Bartholomae, Studien zur idg. sprachgeschichte 2, Halle 1891, 94 sqq.):

idg. **édno-m*: skr. *ánna-m*, food, rice, cf. gr. ἐδανός from **edənó-s*.

idg. **bhidnó-s*: skr. *bhinná-s*, split: *bhinádmi*, I split.

idg. **tudnó-s*: skr. *tunná-s*, pushed: *tudámi*, I push.

Finally it should be mentioned, that skr. *dj* became *jj*.
An instance of this rule is ved. *újjiti-ṣ,* victory, from *ud-*
and *jiti-ṣ.*

§ 51. **Idg. dh.** Idg. *dh* = skr. *dh.*

idg. **dhérsō*: skr. *dhárṣāmi,* I dare, cf. gr. θρασύς, θαρρέω,
Θερσίτης, goth. *gadars.*

idg. **dhūmó-s*: skr. *dhūmá-s,* smoke, gr. θῦμός, lat. *fūmus.*

idg. **dhəi̯b* (root **dhēi̯-*): skr. *dháyāmi,* I suck, goth. *daddja,*
cf. gr. θῆσθαι, θήσατο, lat. *fēlāre, fēmina,* ohg. *tāan.* To the
same root belongs idg. **dhēlu-s*: ved. *dhārú-ṣ,* sucking, gr. θῆλυς.

idg. **dhidhēmi*: skr. *dádhāmi,* I put (instead of **didhāmi*),
gr. τίθημι, cf. ags. *dón.*

idg. **médhu*: skr. *mádhu,* honey, gr. μέθυ, ohg. *meto.*

idg. **k̂ludhí*: ved. *çrudhí,* hear, imperat. of *çṛṇómi,* I hear,
gr. κλύω &c.

idg. **médhi̯o-s*: skr. *mádhya-s,* middle, gr. μέσος, lat. *medius,*
goth. *midjis.*

In certain cases *zdh* became *ždh* in Aryan, from which
skr. *ḍh* (see § 63).

idg. **mizdhó-*: ved. *mīḍhá-m,* prize, contest, gr. μισθός,
cf. goth. *mizdō.*

Idg. *dhn* remained unchanged in Indian:

idg. **bhudhnó-s*: ved. *budhná-s,* bottom, cf. gr. πυθμήν, πύνδαξ,
lat. *fundus* and ohg. *bodam.*

When followed by an aspirate, *dh* lost its aspiration:

idg. **dhidhēmi*: skr. *dádhāmi,* I put, gr. τίθημι.

Idg. *dh* + *t* is represented by *ddh:* see § 49.

In many Sanskrit words and forms, when *dh* might be
expected, we find however *h.* Instances:

idg. **-dhi,* ved. *-dhi, -hi,* skr. *-hi,* suff. 2 pers. sing. imperat. act., gr. -θι.

idg. *-medhai, *-medhə: ved. & skr. -mahe, -mahi, suff. 1 pers. plur. med., avest. -maiδē, gr. -μεθα.

Cf. von Bradke (Zeitschr. der D. Morgenl. Ges. 40, 657 sqq.), who explains ·such cases by Prācritic influence.

Guttural explosives.

§ 52. **General remarks.** A few years ago only two series of gutturals were assumed, viz. a palatal and a velar series. Bezzenberger (Bezz. Beitr. 16, 234 sqq.) has proved, that there was a third series — different from the palatals and velars —, which may be called the *middle* gutturals. In the western Indogermanic languages, viz. in Greek, Italic, Germanic and Celtic, the velars were labialized and the middle gutturals have fallen together with the palatals. In Aryan, Armenian, Phrygian-Thracian, Albanian and Balto-Slavonic the velars were not labialized, but have fallen together with the middle gutturals: here the palatals were changed to spirants. The velars and middle gutturals being represented in Aryan by *one* series, it is preferable not to separate them in a book on Sanskrit phonetics.

§ 53. **The palatalization-rule.** The palatalization-rule concerns the velars and middle gutturals in general: therefore it is to be treated in a separate paragraph, the more so as the discovery of this rule has had a decisive influence on the modern vowel-theories. It has been the strongest, if not the only argument for adopting, that the multiplicity of vowels in the European languages and in Armenian is more original than the Aryan simplicity.

This rule, which was discovered by several scholars at the same time (see Schmidt, Kuhn's Zeitschr. 25, 1—179), may be formulated as follows:

During the Aryan period, before the change of *ĕ* to *ă*, the gutturals (idg. middle gutturals and velars), were palatalized and changed to palatal affricates, when followed by idg. *ĕ*, *ĭ*, *i̭*, and were preserved as gutturals in any other position (cf. however Meillet, Mém. de la Soc. de Ling. 9, 376 sqq.).

Instances of skr. *c, j, h* (from *jh*), going back on gutturals before *ĕ, ĭ, i̭*:

idg. **qe*: skr. *ca*, and, gr. τε, lat. *que*.

idg. **qeru-s*, skr. *carú-ṣ*, kettle, pot, icel. *hverr*.

idg. **qetu̯ǒres*: skr. *catváras*, four, goth. *fidwōr*, cf. gr. τέσσαρες, lat. *quatuor*.

idg. **péṅqe*: skr. *páñca*, five, gr. πέντε, lat. *quinque*, goth. *fimf*.

idg. **léu̯ketai̭*: skr. *rócate*, shines, pleases, cf. gr. λευκός, lat. *lūcet*, goth. *liuhaþ*.

idg. **ǵéretai̭*: ved. *járate*, crackles, invokes, cf. ohg. *quirit*.

idg. **áu̯ges-*: skr. *ójas*, strength, power, cf. *ugrá-s*, mighty, terrible and lat. *augeō*, goth. *aukan*.

idg. **ǵhénmi*: skr. *hánmi*, I slay, cf. gr. θείνω.

idg. **ǵhéros*: ved. *háras*, heat, gr. θέρος.

idg. **-qiti-s*: skr. *ápa-citi-ṣ*, reward, homage, punishment, gr. ἀπό-τισις, τίσις.

idg. **qid*: skr. *cid*, -cunque, gr. τί, lat. *quid*.

idg. **ḱuki-s*: skr. *çúci-ṣ*, light, clear, pure, cf. *çukrá-s*, clear, bright.

idg. **ḱi̭éu̯etai̭*: skr. *cyávate*, moves, falls, cf. gr. σεύω.

Instances of gutturals, which were not followed by *ĕ, ĭ, i̭* and therefore remained unchanged:

idg. **kakŭd-*: skr. *kakút (d)*, *kakúdmān (nt)*, top, summit, lat. *cacūmen* (from **cacūdmen*).

idg. **kark-*: skr. *karká-s*, *karkaṭa-s*, crab, gr. καρκίνος, lat. *cancer* (from **carcer* or **carcen*).

idg. *skandŏ: skr. *skándāmi*, I spring, lat. *scandō*.

idg. *kālo-s: skr. *kāla-s*, dark, black, cf. gr. κηλίς (*κᾱλίς), spot, κηλάς (*κᾱλάς), „νεφέλη ἄνυδρος καὶ χειμερινὴ ἡμέρα", lat. *cālīgo*, mist, darkness.

idg. *kāru-s: ved. *kārú-ṣ*, praiser, singer, cf. gr. κήρῡξ, dor. κᾱρῡξ.

idg. *qā̆setai̯: skr. *kásate*, coughs, cf. ags. *hwósta*, dutch *hoest*. That the radical vowel was *ā* (not *ō*), is seen from lith. *kosėti*, to cough.

idg. *ég̑āt: skr. *ágāt*, went, gr. ἔβη, dor. ἔβᾱ.

idg. *qotero-s: skr. *katará-s*, who (from two), gr. πότερος, ion. κότερος, goth. *hwaþar*.

idg. *kŏ́kso-s, *kŏ́ksā: skr. *kákṣa-s*, region of the girth, girdle &c., underwood, *kákṣā*, girdle, circular wall, lat. *coxa*, mhg. *hahse*.

idg. *jugó-m: skr. *yugá-m*, yoke, age, gr. ζυγόν, lat. *jugum*, goth. *juk*.

idg. *g̑hono-s: skr. *ghaná-s*, slayer (ved.), compact &c., gr. φόνος: skr. *hánmi*, I slay, gr. θείνω.

idg. *dəlghó-s: skr. *dīrghá-s*, long, cf. gr. δολιχός.

idg. *g̑ŏu̯-s: skr. *gáu-ṣ*, cow, gr. βοῦς &c.

idg. *gərú-s: skr. *gurú-ṣ*, heavy, important, worthy of honor, cf. gr. βαρύς, goth. *kaúrus* and lat. *gravis*.

idg. *gərí-s: skr. *girí-ṣ*, mountain, cf. lith. *giria*, forest, oslav. *gora*, mountain.

idg. *gm̥tó-s: skr. *gatá-s*, gone, gr. βατός, lat. *-ventus*.

idg. *i̯ēqr̥-t: skr. *yákr̥t* (*yákr̥t, cf. avest. *yākarĕ*), liver, gr. ἧπαρ, lat. *jecur*.

idg. *kréu̯əs: ved. *kravíṣ*, raw flesh, gr. κρέας, cf. lat. *cruor* and ags. *hréa*, icel. *hrár*.

idg. *k̑ukró-s, *k̑ukló-s: skr. *çukrá-s* (very common in Vedic), *çuklá-s*, clear, bright, white, cf. comparat. *çóciyän* (*ṁs*) and *çúci-ṣ*, light, clear, pure.

idg. **ugró-s*: skr. *ugrá-s*, mighty, terrible, cf. comparat. *ójīyān* (*ṁs*), akin to lat. *augeō*, goth. *aukan* &c.

idg. **stighnutai̯*: skr. *stighnuté*, ascends (Dhātup. *āskandane*), cf. gr. στείχω, goth. *steiga*.

idg. **peṅqti-s*: skr. *paṅktí-ṣ*, row of five, row, cf. gr. πέμπτος.

idg. **siséqti*: ved. *síṣakti*, follows, accompanies, cf. *sácate*, gr. ἕπεται, lat. *sequitur*.

§ 54. **Idg. q, k.** In Aryan the idg. *q* and *k* have fallen together. Before palatal vowels and the semivowel *i̯* they were palatalized, in all other cases they are represented by *k*.

Instances of idg. *q*, *k*, skr. *k*:

idg. **qásetai̯*: skr. *kásate*, coughs, cf. ags. *hwósta*.

idg. **qotero-s*: skr. *katará-s*, who (from two), gr. πότερος, ion. κότερος, goth. *hwaþar*.

idg. **i̯ēqr̥-t*: skr. *yákṛt* (**yákṛt*), gr. ἧπαρ, lat. *jecur*.

idg. **peṅqti-s*: skr. *paṅktí-ṣ*, row of five, row, cf. gr. πέμπτος.

idg. **kakŭd-*: skr. *kakút* (*d*), *kakúdmān* (*nt*), top, summit, lat. *cacūmen*.

idg. **kark-*: skr. *karká-s*, *karkaṭa-s*, crab, gr. καρκίνος, lat. *cancer*.

idg. **kókso-s*, **kóksā*: skr. *kákṣa-s*, region of the girth &c., *kákṣā*, girdle, circular wall, lat. *coxa*, mhg. *hahse*.

idg. **kréu̯əs*: ved. *kravíṣ*, raw flesh, gr. κρέας, cf. lat. *cruor* &c.

Instances of idg. *q*, *k*, skr. *c*:

idg. **qeru-s*: skr. *carú-ṣ*, kettle, pot, icel. *hverr*.

idg. **qetu̯óres*: skr. *catváras*, four, goth. *fidwōr*, cf. gr. τέσσαρες, lat. *quatuor*.

idg. **peṅqe*: skr. *páñca*, five, gr. πέντε, lat. *quinque*, goth. *fimf*.

idg. *qid: skr. cid, -cunque, gr. τί, lat. quid.

idg. *léu̯ketai̯: skr. rócate, shines, pleases, cf. gr. λευκός, lat. lūcet, goth. liuhaþ.

idg. *k̑uki-s: skr. çúci-ṣ, light, clear, pure, cf. çukrá-s, bright, light, clear.

idg. *ki̯éu̯etai̯: skr. cyávate, moves, falls, cf. gr. σεύω.

§ 55. **Idg. qh, k̑h.** Certain examples of idg. qh, k̑h are very rare:

idg. *sqhalṓ: skr. skhálāmi, I stumble, cf. gr. σφάλλω (*sqhl̥i̯ō)?

idg. *k̑oṅkho-s: skr. çaṅkhá-s, shell, gr. κόγχος, cf. lat. congius.

Instances of skr. kh, iran. χ:

skr. khára-, ass, avest. χara-.

skr. khá-s, well, avest. χan-, χāo.

skr. sákhā, friend, avest. haχa.

In skr. kumbhá-, pot, the initial k was originally aspirated, cf. avest. χumba-. The loss of the h was caused by dissimilation.

Concerning the combination cch (ch) it is not yet certain, whether it should be explained from idg. skh before palatal vowels or from idg. sk̑h. In the former case gácchāmi, icchámi, pr̥cchámi would have cch by analogy, because idg. *gm̥skhṓ, *isskhṓ, *pr̥k̑skhṓ would have given *gaskhāmi, *iṣkhāmi, *pr̥ṣkhāmi; the cch of gácchatī, iccháti, pr̥ccháti regularly would represent the idg. skh before idg. e: idg. *gm̥skhéti, *isskhéti, *pr̥k̑skhéti. In the latter case gácchāmi, icchámi, pr̥cchámi also would be organic forms. Cf. on this question Zubatý, Kuhn's Zeitschr. 31, 9 sqq. and Bartholomae, Studien zur idg. sprachgeschichte 2, 3 sqq. Instances:

skr. chinádmi, I cut off, cf. avest. sid- (s from sk̑), gr. σχίζω, lat. scindō, lith. skëdžiu (lith. idg. sk̑).

skr. *chāyá*' shade, shadow, cf. pers. *sāya* (*s* from *sk̂*), gr.
σκιά, oslav. *stěnĭ* from **scěnĭ*, **skěnĭ* (slav. idg. *sk*).

skr. *iccháti*, wishes, cf. avest. *isaiti* (*s* from *sk̂*), lith. *jĕsz-koti*, oslav. *iskati* (lith. *szk*, slav. *sk*, idg. *sk*), ohg. *eiscōn*.

skr. *gácchati*, goes, cf. avest. *jasaiti* (*s* from *sk̂*), gr. βάσκω.

skr. *pṛccháti*, asks, cf. avest. *pĕrĕsaiti* (*s* from *sk̂*), lat. *poscō*, ohg. *forscōn*.

§ 56. **Idg.** *ǵ*, **g**. In Aryan the idg. *ǵ* and *g* have fallen together. Before palatal vowels and the semivowel *i̯* they were palatalized, in all other cases they are represented by *g*.

Instances of idg. *ǵ*, *g*, skr. *g*:

idg. **ǵŏu̯-s*: skr. *gáu-ṣ*, cow, gr. βοῦς &c.

idg. **ǵərú-s*: skr. *gurú-ṣ*, heavy, cf. gr. βαρύς, goth. *kaúrus* (and lat. *gravis*).

idg. **éǵāt*: skr. *ágāt*, went, gr. ἔβη.

idg. **ǵṃtó-s*: skr. *gatá-s*, gone, gr. βατός, lat. *-ventus*.

idg. **jugó-m*: skr. *yugá-m*, yoke, age, gr. ζυγόν, lat. *jugum*, goth. *juk*.

idg. **ugró-s*: skr. *ugrá-s*, mighty, terrible, cf. lat. *augeō*, goth. *aukan*.

Instances of idg. *ǵ*, *g*, skr. *j*:

idg. **ǵéretai̯*: ved. *járate*, crackles, invokes, cf. ohg. *quirit*.

idg. **au̯ges-*: skr. *ójas-*, strength, power, cf. *ugrá-s*, mighty, terrible, lat. *augeō*, goth. *aukan*.

§ 57. **Idg.** *ǵh*, **gh**. In Aryan the idg. *ǵh* and *gh* have fallen together. Before palatal vowels and the semivowel *i̯* they became *jh*, in all other cases they are represented by *gh*. In Indian *jh* became *h*.

Instances of idg. *ǵh*, *gh*, skr. *gh*:

idg. **ghono-s*: skr. *ghaná-s*, slayer (ved.), compact &c., gr. φόνος, cf. ohg. *gundea*, ags. *gúđ*.

idg. *dəlghó-s: skr. dīrghá-s, long, cf. gr. δολιχός.

idg. *stighnutai̯: skr. stighnuté, ascends, cf. gr. στείχω, goth. steiga.

Instances of idg. ₰h, gh, skr. h:

idg. *₰hénmi: skr. hánmi, I slay, cf. gr. θείνω.

idg. *₰héros: ved. háras, heat, gr. θέρος.

idg. *dhrughes: ved. drúhas, harming spirits, cf. skr. drúh-yāmi, I harm, avest. druj-, ohg. triogan.

When followed by an aspirate, gh (ǰh) lost its aspiration:

idg. *ghr̥dhi̯ō: skr. gŕdhyāmi, I am eager, cf. goth. grēdus, grēdags·

idg. *₰he₰hóna: skr. jaghána, I have slain: hánmi, I slay, gr. θείνω.

Idg. ₰h + t and gh + t are represented by gdh: see § 49.

Palatal explosives.

§ 58. **General remarks.** Besides the velars and middle gutturals there was a third series of guttural explosives, formed at the foremost part of the hard palate. These foremost gutturals are called palatals. In Aryan, Armenian, Phrygian-Thracian, Albanian and Balto-Slavonic the palatal explosives were changed to palatal spirants: in the same dialect-groups the velars and middle gutturals fell together into one series of guttural explosives. In Greek, Italic, Germanic and Celtic, where the velars were labialized, the palatals fell together with the middle gutturals. According to the manner, in which the gutturals were treated, the Indogermanic languages may be divided into two groups, a western, where the difference between palatals and middle gutturals has been effaced, and an eastern, where the velars have fallen together with the middle gutturals, but where the palatal explosives have become spirants. Von Bradke has called the western group that of the *centum*-languages, the eastern group that of the *satĕm*-languages. It may be supposed, that the *centum*-languages descend from an other dialect of the mother-tongue than the *satĕm*-languages. Cf. von Bradke, Ueber methode und ergehnisse der arischen alterthumswissenschaft (Giessen 1890), 63.

§ 59. **Idg. k̂.** During the Aryan period the idg. *k̂* became *ç*. This voiceless palatal spirant remained unchanged in Indian:

idg. *k̂m̥tó-m: skr. *çatá-m*, hundred, gr. *ἑ-κατόν*, lat. *centum*, goth. *hund*, lith. *szimtas* (cf. § 18).

idg. *k̂aṅkú-s: skr. *çaṅkú-ṣ*, wedge, stake, oslav. *sǫkŭ*, branch, cf. skr. *çā́khā*, branch, lith. *szaka* (also goth. *hōha?*).

idg. *k̂énsō: skr. *çáṁsāmi*, I recite, I praise, I announce, cf. lat. *censeō*.

idg. *k̂ūro-s: skr. *çū́ra-s*, mighty, bold, hero, gr. *-κῡρος* in *ἄ-κῡρος*, not valid.

idg. *k̂u̯ó(n): skr. *çvá* (n), dog, lith. *szŭ*, with *n* gr. *κύων*, cf. goth. *hunds*.

idg. *su̯ek̂uro-s: skr. *çváçura-s*. father in law, gr. *ἑκυρός*, cf. lat. *socer* and goth. *swaíhra*. Oslav. *svekrŭ* has idg. *k* or *q*; on the contrary lith. *szeszuras* regularly has *sz* from *k̂*. The feminine of *su̯ek̂uro-s is *su̯ek̂rū́-s: skr. *çvaçrū́-ṣ*, mother in law, lat. *socrus*, oslav. *svekry* (with *k* as *svekrŭ*), cf. gr. *ἑκυρά* (probably an analogous formation to *ἑκυρός*) and goth. *swaíhrō*.

idg. *u̯ói̯k̂o-s: skr. *veça-s*, house, gr. *οἶκος*, lat. *vicus*, cf. goth. *weihs*.

idg. *dn̥k̂ó: skr. *dáçāmi*, I bite, cf. gr. *δάκνω* (also ohg. *zangar*, sharp).

idg. *ák̂ru: skr. *áçru*, tear, cf. *açrá-m* (of course to be written with *ç*, not with *s*), tear, lith. *aszara* (with an initial *d* gr. *δάκρυ*, lat. *lacruma*, goth. *tagr*).

idg. *$a\hat{k}m\bar{o}(n)$: ved. *áçmā* (*n*), stone, gr. ἄκμων, lith. pl. tantum *aszmens*, edge, but with *k* or *q* lith. *akmů*, oslav. *kamy*, stone (cf. ohg. *hamar*, icel. *hamarr*, originally, „a weapon of stone"?).

idg. *$ded\acute{o}r\hat{k}a$: skr. *dadárça*, I have seen, gr. δέδορκα.

The idg. combination $\hat{k}t$ regularly became *çt* in Aryan, that is represented in Indian by *ṣṭ*:

idg. *$o\hat{k}t\acute{o}(u)$: skr. *aṣṭá* (ved.), *aṣṭáu*, eight, gr. ὀκτώ, lat. *octō*, goth. *ahtau*.

idg. *$di\hat{k}ti$-s: skr. *diṣṭi-ṣ*, indication, prescription, destiny, ohg. *-ziht* in *inziht*, accusation, cf. lat. *dictiō* and with strong vocalism gr. δεῖξις.

idg. *$\underset{\,}{u}\acute{e}\hat{k}ti$: skr. *váṣṭi*, is willing, cf. *uçánt-*, willing, gr. ἑκών. The first person is *váçmi* from *$\underset{\,}{u}\acute{e}\hat{k}mi$.

Brugmann 1, 299 assumes, that $s\hat{k}$ became *cch* (*ch*) in Indian: cf. however § 55 and § 62.

The idg. combination $\hat{k}s$ is represented by *kṣ*:

idg. *$\underset{\,}{u}\acute{e}\hat{k}si$: skr. *vákṣi*, thou art willing, cf. *váçmi*, I am willing, gr. ἑκών.

idg. *$d\acute{e}\hat{k}sino$-s: skr. *dákṣiṇa-s*, right, southern, clever, able, oslav. *desĭnŭ*, lith. *deszinė* (fem. of the *ė*-class, right hand), cf. gr. δεξιός, lat. *dexter*, goth. *taíhswa*.

§ 60. **Idg. $\hat{g}$.** During the Aryan period the idg. *ĝ* became a voiced palatal spirant (*ž*), which was changed in Indian to an affricate (*dž*, written *j*):

idg. *$\hat{g}\acute{e}nos$: ved. *jánas*, race, family, gr. γένος, lat. *genus*, cf. goth. *kuni*: skr. *janáyāmi*, I beget, I produce, gr. γίγνομαι, lat. *gignō* &c. Avest. *zan-* proves, that the *j* of *janáyāmi* is an idg. *ĝ*.

idg. *$\hat{g}\acute{o}nu$: skr. *jánu*, knee, cf. gr. γόνυ, lat. *genu* and with loss of the root-vowel ved. *jñu-* in *jñu-bádh-*, bending the knees, gr. *γνυ-* in *γνυπετεῖν*, goth. *kniu*. Avest. *zanva*, knees.

idg. **ĝnōtó-s*: skr. *jñātá-s*, known, gr. *γνωτός*, lat. *nōtus*: skr. *jānā́mi*, I know, gr. *γιγνώσκω*, lat. *nōscō (gnōscō)*, cf. ags. *cnáwan*, ohg. *chnāan* (with idg. *ē*) and ohg. *einchnuadil, cnuodelen*. That we have to do with idg. *ĝ*, appears from lith. *žinoti*, oslav. *znati* &c.

idg. **ĝusó*: skr. *juṣā́mi*, I take pleasure, I relish, cf. idg. **ĝéu̯sō*, gr. *γεύω*, goth. *kiusa* and idg. **ĝustu-s*, lat. *gustus*, goth. *kustus*. Avest. *zaoša-* (= skr. *jóṣa-*), wish.

idg. **bhərĝo-s*: skr. *bhūrja-s*, birch, cf. ohg. *pirihha*. The *ĝ* appears from oslav. *bréza*, lith. *beržas*.

idg. **mr̥ĝó*: skr. *mr̥jā́mi*, I rub, wipe, strip, cf. gr. *ἀμέλγω*, lat. *mulgeō*, ohg. *milchu* &c. Lith. *melžu*, oslav. *mlŭzą* prove, that we have *ĝ*.

The idg. combination *ĝb(h)* regularly became in Aryan *žb(h)*, from which skr. *ḍb(h)*: cf. § 63. Example:

idg. **u̯iĝbhís*: skr. *viḍbhíṣ*, instrum. pl. of *viç-*, nom. *viṭ*, settlement, community, clan, tribe, people, cf. gr. *οῖκος*, lat. *vīcus* &c.

§ 61. **Idg. ĝh.** During the Aryan period the idg. *ĝh* became *žh*. This aspirated spirant is in general represented by skr. *h*. The intermediate *jh* is preserved in skr. *ujjhitá-s*, left, from **ud-jhita-s*: *jáhāmi*, I leave (*ujjhāmi* has been formed by analogy). Instances of idg. *ĝh*, skr. *h*:

idg. **ĝhéi̯men-*: ved. *héman-*, winter, gr. *χεῖμα, χειμών*, cf. skr. *himá-m*, snow, gr. *χιών*, lat. *hiems*. The *ĝh* appears from lith. *žёma*, oslav. *zima* &c.

idg. **ĝhansó-s*: skr. *haṁsá-s*, goose, swan, cf. gr. *χήν*, lat. *anser*, ohg. *gans*. Lith. *žąsis* proves, that we have *ĝh*; surprising is the *g* of oslav. *gąsĭ* (perhaps an ancient loan from Germanic).

idg. *$lé\underset{.}{i}ghmi$: skr. *léhmi*, I lick, cf. gr. λείχω, lat. *lingō*, goth. *-laigōn*. The *ĝh* appears from lith. *lëžiu*, oslav. *ližǫ* &c.

idg. *$bhāĝhu$-s*: skr. *bāhú-ṣ*, arm, gr. πῆχυς, ohg. *buog*. Avest. *bāzu-*.

idg. *$\underset{.}{u}éĝhō$*: skr. *váhāmi*, I carry, lat. *vehō*, goth. *-wiga*. Lith. *vežu*, oslav. *vezǫ* &c. prove, that we have to do with *ĝh*.

Idg. *ĝh* + *t* became skr. *ḍh*, sometimes with modification of a preceding vowel:

idg. *$lé\underset{.}{i}ĝh$-ti*: skr. *léḍhi*, licks, cf. gr. λείχω.

idg. *$liĝh$-tós*: skr. *līḍhá-s*, licked: *léḍhi*.

idg. *$uĝh$-tó-s*: skr. *ūḍhá-s*, carried: *váhāmi*, I carry.

idg. *$dh\underset{.}{r}ĝh$-tó-s*: skr. *dṛḍhá-s*, firm: *dṛ́hyāmi*, *dṛ́mhāmi*, I make firm.

idg. *$sēĝh$-tó-s*: skr. *sāḍhá-s*, overpowered &c.: *sáhāmi*, I overpower, 1 withstand &c., gr. ἔχω.

idg. *$\underset{.}{u}éĝh$-tum*: skr. *vóḍhum*, to carry: *váhāmi*, I carry.

idg. *$séĝh$-tum*: skr. *sóḍhum*, to withstand &c.: *sáhāmi*, I withstand &c.

When followed by an aspirate, *ĝh* became *j*:

idg. *$ĝhiĝhāmi$*: skr. *jáhāmi*, I leave. The *i* of the reduplication-syllable was replaced by *a* before the end of the Aryan period, cf. avest. *zazāiti*, leaves.

Spirants.

§ 62. **Idg. s.** In general the idg. *s* remained unchanged:

idg. *$sept\underset{.}{n}$*: skr. *saptá*, seven, gr. ἑπτά, lat. *septem*, cf. goth. *sibun*. Lith. *septyni* proves, that we have to do with *ṇ*, not with *ṃ*.

idg. *$séno$-s*: ved. *sána-s*, old, gr. fem. ἔνη, cf. lat. *senex*, goth. *sineigs*.

idg. *sréu̯ō: skr. *srávāmi*, I flow, I stream, gr. *ῥέω*, cf. ohg. *stroum*.

idg. *véstai̯: skr. *váste*, clothes one's self, puts on, cf. *vásana-m*, *vástra-m*, garment, gr. *ἕννῡμι*, *ἑανός*, *ἐσθής*, lat. *vestis*, goth. *wasjan*, *wasti*.

idg. *dōsi̯ō: skr. *dāsyámi*, gr. *δώσω*.

idg. *ǵénos, gen. *ǵénesos: ved. *jánas*, gen. *jánasas*, race, family, gr. *γένος*, lat. *genus*.

idg. *éḱu̯o-s: skr. *áçva-s*, horse, gr. *ἵππος*, lat. *equus*, germ. *éχwoz, icel. *jór*, ags. *eoh*.

Already during the Aryan period *s* was changed to *š* after *ĭ*, *ŭ*, *i̯*, *u̯*, *r̥*, *r*, *q*, *k*, *ḱ*. In the same conditions *ss* became *šš*. In Indian the *š* is lingualized and *šš* has become *kṣ* (cf. however Wackernagel 1, 137). I can not agree with Hirt (Idg. forschungen 4, 44), Zubatý (Arch. f. slav. phil. 16, 404 note), Pedersen (Idg. forschungen 5, 33 sqq.) and Wackernagel 1, 231, who assume a connection between the Aryan change of *s* to *š* and the Slavonic transition of *s* to *ch* (see Arch. f. slav. phil. 16, 368 sqq.; Museum 4, 50).

idg. *sthisthāmi: skr. *tíṣṭhāmi*, I stand, gr. *ἵστημι*, cf. lat. *sistō*.

idg. *ustó-s: skr. *uṣṭá-s*, burned, lat. *ustus*.

idg. *u̯l̥qoi̯su: skr. *vŕ̥keṣu*, loc. plur. of *vŕ̥ka-s,* wolf, oslav. *vlŭcéchŭ*.

idg. *ǵeu̯ster-: ved. *joṣṭár-*, *jóṣṭar-*, loving, cf. gr. *γευστήριον*.

idg. *du̯éi̯ssi: skr. *dvékṣi* (from *dváišš(i)*, thou hatest, 2 pers. of *dvéṣmi*.

idg. *sau̯ssi̯ō: skr. *çokṣyámi* (from *sau̯ššyámi*), I shall dry up, gr. *αὔσω*.

idg. *dhr̥snéu̯mi, *dhérsō: skr. *dhr̥ṣṇómi*, *dhárṣāmi*, I dare, cf. gr. *θαρρέω* &c.

idg. *kərs-: skr. *çirṣá-m*, *çirṣán-*, head, cf. *çíras*, head, gr. κόρση (κόρρη), κέρας, κάρᾱ, lat: *cerebrum*, *cernuus*, icel. *hjarne*, *hjarse*, ohg. *hirni*.

idg. *uersā: skr. *varṣá*, rain, gr. ἔρση, ἔρση.

idg. *ueqsiō: skr. *vakṣyámi*, I shall say: *vácmi*, I say, cf. *vák*, voice, lat. *vōx* &c.

idg. *dheksiō: skr. *dhakṣyámi*, I shall burn: *dáhāmi*, I burn, lith. *degu*, cf. goth. *dags*.

idg. * uéksi: skr. *vákṣi*, thou art willing, cf. *váçmi*, I am willing, gr. ἑκών.

It is to be noticed, that skr. *ṣ* was turned back into *s*, when immediately followed by *r̥* or *r*:

idg. *tisres, *tisr̥bhis &c.: skr. *tisrás*, fem. three, instrum. *tisr̥bhiṣ*, cf. avest. *tišarō*, irish *teora*.

Brugmann 1, 412 and Bartholomae (Studien zur idg. sprach-geschichte 2, 5) assume, that the idg. *sq*, *sk* before palatal vowels became *çc* in Aryan, cf. ved. *paçcá*, behind, later, west, avest. *pasca* (originally an instrumental, ending in idg. *ē*). Against this opinion Meillet, Mém. de la Soc. de Ling. 9, 375 sq.

It would seem, that the idg. *sqh*, *skh* before palatal vowels are represented in Indian by *cch* (*ch*), but Bartholomae (Studien zur idg. sprachgeschichte 2, 3 sqq.) has tried to prove, that *cch* (*ch*) goes back on a combination of *k̂*. Cf. § 55, where examples of *cch* are given.

The idg. *ss* after *a*-vowels became *ts* in Indian. In most cases however *ss* had been simplified before the end of the Indogermanic period, cf. skr. *ási*, thou art, avest. *ahi*, gr. εἶ, idg. *ési from *és-si. Instances of idg. *ss*, skr. *ts*:

idg. *vessiō: skr. *vatsyámi*, I shall put on, gr. ἔσσω, fut. of idg. *ves-.

idg. *_yessi̯ō_: skr. _vatsyāmi_, I shall dwell, fut. of _vásāmi_, I dwell, goth. _wisan_.

idg. *_yidu̯éssu_: skr. _vidvátsu_, loc. pl. of _vidvân_, knowing, wise, cf. gr. εἰδώς and goth. _weitwōps_.

Between explosives _s_ was lost: _utthátum_, to stand up, to rise up, from *_utsthátum_ (_ud_ + _sthátum_); _átāpta_, you were warm, from *_átāpsta_ (aor. of _tápāmi_).

In the neighbourhood of _ç_ and _ṣ_ the idg. _s_ became assimilated to _ç_:

idg. *_su̯eḱuro-s_: skr. _çváçura-s_, father in law, gr. ἑκυρός, cf. with a similar assimilation lith. _szeszuras_.

idg. *_smaḱru_: skr. _çmáçru_, beard, cf. lith. _smakra_, chin (with idg. _k_), and perhaps lat. _maxilla_.

idg. *_suskó-s_: skr. _çuṣká-s_, dry, avest. _huška-_, cf. lith. _sausas_, oslav. _suchŭ_, ohg. _sōr_.

idg. *_ḱasó-s_: skr. _çaçá-s_, hare, cf. ohg. _haso_, ags. _hara_, opruss. _sasnis_.

§ 63. **Idg.** **z.** Osthoff (Kuhn's Zeitschr. 23, 87—89) has proved, that during the Indogermanic period _s_ before voiced consonants had become voiced. In Aryan this voiced sibilant (_z_) was preserved after _a_-vowels, but changed to _ž_ after _r̥_, _u̥_, _i̥_, _u̯_. In Indian the _ž_ became lingual. Afterwards it disappeared in any position, as well as the unchanged _z_.

Idg. _azd(h)_, _ezd(h)_, _ozd(h)_ = ar. _azd(h)_ = skr. _ed(h)_:

idg. *_sezdi̯ēt_: ved. _sedyát_, 3 pers. sing. optat. perf. of the root _sad-_, to sit, avest. _hazdyāp_.

idg. *_ezdhí_, *_zdhi_: skr. _edhí_, imperat. of the root _as-_, to be, avest. _zdī_, cf. gr. ἴσθι.

Idg. _āzd(h)_, _ēzd(h)_, _ōzd(h)_ = ar. _āzd(h)_ = skr. _ād(h)_:

idg. *_ēzdhu̯ai̯_: skr. _ádhve_, you sit, cf. _áste_, sits, gr. ἧσται.

idg. *$k\bar{a}zdh\acute{i}$: skr. $\varphi\bar{a}dh\acute{i}$, imperat. of the root $\varphi\bar{a}s$-, to rule, to punish &c.

Idg. $zd(h)$ after $\bar{\imath}$, $\bar{u}$, $\rlap{/}{\imath}$, $\rlap{/}{u}$ = ar. $\dot{z}d(h)$ = skr. $\rlap{.}{d}(h)$:

idg. *$nizd\acute{o}$-s: skr. $n\bar{\imath}\rlap{.}{d}\acute{a}$-$s$, nest, lat. $n\bar{\imath}dus$, ohg. $nest$.

idg. *$duzd\bar{e}k$-: ved. $d\bar{u}\rlap{.}{d}\acute{a}\varphi$-, not pious, cf. skr. $du\rlap{.}{s}$-, gr. $\delta\upsilon\varsigma$-, goth. tuz-.

idg. *$\acute{e}sta\rlap{/}{u}zdh\rlap{/}{u}am$: ved. $\acute{a}sto\rlap{.}{d}hvam$, 2 pers. plur. aor. med. of $st\acute{a}umi$, I praise.

Idg. $zb(h)$ after a-vowels = ar. $zb(h)$ = skr. $\rlap{.}{d}b(h)$:

idg. *$\rlap{/}{u}id\rlap{/}{u}ezbhis$: skr. $vidv\acute{a}dbhi\rlap{.}{s}$, instrum. pl. of $vidv\acute{a}n$, knowing.

idg. *$m\bar{e}zbhis$: ved. $m\bar{a}dbh\acute{\imath}\rlap{.}{s}$, instrum. pl. of $m\acute{a}s$, moon, month.

Idg. $zb(h)$ after $\bar{\imath}$, $\bar{u}$, $\rlap{/}{\imath}$, $\rlap{/}{u}$ = ar. $\dot{z}b(h)$ = $\rlap{.}{d}b(h)$:

idg. *$d\rlap{/}{u}izbh\acute{\imath}s$: skr. $dvi\rlap{.}{d}bh\acute{\imath}\rlap{.}{s}$, instrum. pl. of $dvi\rlap{.}{s}$-, nom. $dvi\rlap{.}{t}$, hating.

idg. *$\rlap{/}{u}ipruzbh\acute{\imath}s$: skr. $vipr\acute{u}\rlap{.}{d}bhi\rlap{.}{s}$, instrum. pl. of $vipr\acute{u}\rlap{.}{s}$-, nom. $vipr\acute{u}\rlap{.}{t}$, crumb, spot, spark.

Idg. $zg(h)$ after a-vowels, not followed by a palatal vowel or $\rlap{/}{\imath}$, = ar. $zg(h)$ = skr. $dg(h)$:

idg. *$mezg\acute{u}$-s: skr. $madg\acute{u}$-$\rlap{.}{s}$, a kind of waterfowl, cf. lat. $mergus$: skr. $m\acute{a}jjati$, see below.

Idg. zg after a-vowels, followed by a palatal vowel, = ar. zj ($zd\check{z}$) = skr. jj:

idg. *$m\acute{e}zgeti$: skr. $m\acute{a}jjati$, sinks under, dives, lat. $mergit$.

Between explosives z is lost in Indian: ved. $\acute{a}mugdhvam$ from *$\acute{a}mugzdhvam$, 2 pers. pl. aor. med. of $mu\tilde{n}c\acute{a}ti$, releases, loosens.

§ 64. **Idg. j.** The idg. spirant j has fallen together with the semivowel $\rlap{/}{\imath}$ in all Indogermanic languages except Greek:

idg. *$jug\acute{o}$-m: skr. $yug\acute{a}$-m, yoke, gr. $\zeta\upsilon\gamma\acute{o}\nu$, lat. $jugum$, goth. juk.

idg. *jésō: skr. *yásāmi* (the common form in literature is *yásyāmi*), I seethe, I boil, gr. ζέω, cf. ohg. *jesan*.

idg. *jéu̯o-s: skr. *yáva-s*, corn, barley, cf. gr. ζειαί, spelt, lith. *javai*, corn.

idg. *jūs-: ved. *yûṣ-, yūṣán-*, skr. *yūṣa-s, yūṣa-m*, broth, lat. *jūs*, oslav. *jucha*, cf. gr. ζύμη.

Perhaps also:

idg. *k̂éjtai̯: skr. *çéte*, lies, gr. κεῖται.

idg. *tjeg̑-: skr. *tyájāmi*, I leave, *tyaktá-s*, left, gr. σέβομαι, σεπτός.

See Brugmann 1, 454. If *çéte* and *tyájāmi* originally contained the semivowel *i̯*, a gradation *çe-*: *çi-, *tyaj-*: *tij-* might have been expected.

§ 65. **Idg.** v. The mother-language seems to have possessed a spirant *v*, which already in Aryan had fallen together with the semivowel *u̯*. The most certain criterion of idg. *v* is the absence of weaker forms containing *u* (Brugmann, 1, 409). Instance:

idg. *véstai̯: skr. *váste*, clothes one's self, puts on, cf. *vásana-m*, *vásma* (*n*), *vástra-m*, garment, gr. ἔννῡμι, ἑανός, εἷμα (lesb. ϝέμμα), ἐσθής, lat. *vestis, vestiō*, goth. *wasjan, wasti*.

§ 66. **Idg.** γ. Von Fierlinger (Kuhn's Zeitschr. 27, 478 note) supposes, that there was a voiced palatal spirant γ in the mother-language, represented by skr. *h*, avest. *z*, gr. γ, lat. *g*, germ. *k*. Though this theory may not claim a high degree of probability, it will be useful to mention the few cases, where skr. *h* seems to correspond to gr. γ &c.:

idg. *γénu-s: skr. *hánu-ṣ*, jaw, gr. γένυς, cf. goth. *kinnus* and lat. *gena*.

idg. *γe: skr. *ha*, enclit. particle, gr. γε, goth. -*k* in *mik*, *þuk*, *sik*.

idg. *γosto-s, *əγosto-s: skr. *hásta-s*, hand, trunk (of an elephant), paw &c., gr. ἀγοστός (see de Saussure 53).

idg. *eγŏm: skr. *ahám*, I, gr. ἐγών, cf. gr. ἐγώ, lat. *ego*, goth. *ik*.

idg. *dhuγətē(r): skr. *duhitá* (r), daughter, gr. θυγάτηρ, cf. goth. *daúhtar*.

idg. *gŭγ-: skr. *gúhāmi*, I hide, cf. Ὠγυγία, Ὤγυγος, Γύγης.

idg. *mèγ-: skr. *mahán* (*nt*), great, cf. ved. *máhi*, nom. acc. neutr. great, adv. very, subst. greatness, gr. μέγα (idg. *méγə).

§ 67. **Idg.** *þ*, *đ*. In general skr. *kṣ* corresponds to gr. ξ, but in some cases we find gr. κτ, χθ or φθ instead of ξ. We must assume, that the skr. *ṣ*, which is represented by gr. τ, θ, goes back on dental sounds, which were different from *s* and from the ordinary idg. dental explosives. Perhaps these dental sounds were spirants (*þ*, *đ*). See Brugmann 1, 409 sq. and Kretschmer, Kuhn's Zeitschr. 31, 429 sqq.

Instances of skr. *kṣ*, gr. κτ, idg. *kþ*, *k̂þ*:

ved. *kṣémi*, I dwell, skr. *kṣétra-m*, field, *kṣití-ṣ*, dwelling, abode, earth, ved. pl. tribes, gr. rhod. κτοίνα, dwelling-place, gr. κτίζω, κτίσις, ἀμφικτίονες, ἐϋκτίμενος. Avest. *šaeiti* proves, that the initial guttural was *k̂*.

ved. *kṣáyāmi*, I possess, gr. κτάομαι, κτῆμα. Avest. *χšayeiti* proves, that the original *anlaut* was *k*.

skr. *kṣaṇómi*, I hurt, gr. κτείνω. Opers. -χšata- = skr. *kṣatá-*.

skr. *ŕkṣa-s*, bear, gr. ἄρκτος, lat. *ursus*. Avest. *arəša-* (?).

skr. *tákṣā* (*n*), carpenter, gr. τέκτων, cf. lat. *texere*. Avest. *taš-*.

Instance of skr. *kṣ*, gr. φθ, idg. *qþh*:

skr. *kṣiṇ́ámi* (ved.), later *kṣiṇómi*, *kṣáyāmi*, I destroy, *kṣíti-ṣ*, destruction, gr. φθίνω, φθίσις. Avest. *χšaya-* proves, that skr. *kṣ*, gr. *φθ* here goes back on a combination of voiceless consonants.

Instances of skr. *kṣ*, gr. *χθ*, *φθ*, idg. *ĝdh*, *g̃dh*:

ved. *kṣá-s*, dwelling-place, earth, pl. *kṣámas*, gr. *χθών*, cf. gr. *χαμαί*, lat. *humus*, avest. *zĕm-*, lith. *žemė*, oslav. *zemlja*, which prove, that skr. *kṣ*, gr. *χθ* here represents an idg. combination of voiced consonants.

skr. *kṣárāmi*, I flow, melt away, perish, gr. *Φθείρω*. Avest. *γžaraiti* proves, that the initial group of consonants was originally voiced.

B. The relation of the Indian consonants to the Indogermanic.

Semivowels.

§ 68. **Skr. y.** In skr. *y* have fallen together the idg. *i̯* and *j*.

Skr. *y* = idg. *i̯*:

skr. *yá-s*, who, gr. *ὅς*.

skr. *yákṛt*, liver, originally **yákṛt*, gr. *ἧπαρ*, lat. *jecur*.

skr. *tráyas*, three, gr. *τρεῖς*, lat. *trēs*, goth. *þreis*.

skr. *mádhya-s*, middle, gr. *μέσος*, lat. *medius*, goth. *midjis*.

skr. *jyá*, bowstring, cf. gr. *βιός*.

Skr. *y* = idg. *j*:

skr. *yugá-m*, yoke, gr. *ζυγόν*, lat. *jugum*, goth. *juk*.

skr. *yásāmi* (*yásyāmi*), I seethe, I boil, gr. *ζέω*, cf. ohg. *jesan*.

skr. *yáva-s*, corn, barley, cf. gr. *ζειαί*, lith. *javai*.

skr. *tyájāmi*, I leave, cf. gr. *σέβομαι*, *σεμνός*.

§ 69. **Skr. v.** In skr. *v* have fallen together the idg. *u̯*
and *v*.

Skr. *v* = idg. *u̯*:

skr. *vácas*, word, *vák*, voice, gr. ἔπος, lat. *vōx*.

skr. *véda*, I know, gr. οἶδα, goth. *wait*.

skr. *veça-s*, house, gr. οἶκος, lat. *vicus*, cf. goth. *weihs*.

skr. *náva-s*, new, gr. νέος, lat. *novus*, cf. ved. *návya-s*, goth.
niujis &c.

skr. *svādú-ṣ*, sweet, gr. ἡδύς, cf. lat. *suāvis* and os. *swōti*.

skr. *sárva-s*, all, gr. ὅλος, οὖλος.

Skr. *v* = idg. *v*:

skr. *váste*, puts on, cf. gr. ἕννῡμι, ἐσθής, lat. *vestis*, goth.
wasjan.

Nasals.

§ 70. **Skr. m.** Skr. *m* = idg. *m*:

skr. *mātá*, mother, gr. μήτηρ, lat. *māter*, ohg. *muoter*.

skr. *mṛti-ṣ*, death, lat. *mors*, cf. goth. *maúrþr*.

skr. *mnāta-s*, mentioned, cf. gr. μιμνήσκω.

skr. *mlā́yāmi*, I wither, cf. gr. βλᾱ́ξ.

skr. *vámāmi*, *vámimi*, I vomit, cf. gr. ἐμέω, lat. *vomō*.

skr. *smáyate*, smiles, cf. gr. φιλομμειδής, μειδιάω, lat.
mīrus, engl. *smile*.

skr. *gharmá-s*, heat, lat. *formus*, ohg. *warm*, cf. gr. θερμός.

ved. *jámbha-s*, set of teeth, tooth, gr. γόμφος, ohg. *chamb*.

skr. *tám*, acc. pron., gr. τόν, lat. *is-tum*, goth. *þan-a*.

§ 71. **Skr. n.** Skr. *n* = idg. *n*:

skr. *náu-ṣ*, ship, gr. ναῦς, cf. lat. *nāvis*, icel. *nó-*.

skr. *nábhas*, sky, gr. νέφος, cf. gr. νεφέλη, lat. *nebula*,
ohg. *nebul*.

skr. *náma (n)*, name, lat. *nōmen*, cf. gr. ὄνομα and goth. *namō*.

ved. *sána-s*, old, gr. fem. *ἔνη*, cf. lat. *senex* and goth. *sineigs*.

ved. *vidmáne*, to know, gr. *ἴδμεναι*.

skr. voc. *tókṣan*, carpenter, gr. *τέκτον*.

In some cases the skr. *n* goes back on idg. *m*:

ved. *gántu*, 3 pers. sing. imperat. of *gam-*, to go. Idg. *mt* became *nt*.

ved. *dán*, of the house, gr. *δες-* in *δεσπότης*, cf. ved. *dáma-s*, gr. *δόμος* &c. At the end of words idg. *ms* became *n*.

§ 72. **Skr. ṇ.** Skr. *ṇ* often goes back on idg. *n*: in most cases the lingualization is due to the influence of neighbouring lingual consonants. In an other group of words *ṇ* is the representative of idg. *ln*.

Skr. *ṇ* = idg. *n*:

skr. *kṛṣṇá-s*, black, opruss. *kirsna-*.

skr. *uṣṇá-s*, hot: *óṣāmi*, gr. *εὔω*, lat. *ūrō*.

ved. *mṛṇámi*, I crush, gr. med. *μάρναμαι*.

skr. *tṛṇa-m*, grass, cf. goth. *paúrnus*.

skr. *dvéṣāṇi*, 1 pers. sing. praes. conj. (imperat.) of *dvéṣmi*, I hate.

skr. *kriṇámi*, I buy, cf. gr. *ἐπριάμην*.

In loans from Prākrit dialects, not in the neighbourhood of linguals:

skr. *maṇí-ṣ*, jewel, os. *meni*, cf. lat. *monile*.

skr. *bhaṇāmi*, I speak, ved. *bhánāmi*.

Skr. *ṇ* = idg. *ln*:

skr. *kiṇa-s*, callosity, lat. *callus* (*callum*).

skr. *kuṇi-ṣ*, lame of one arm, cf. gr. *κυλλός*.

skr. *āṇí-ṣ*, the leg immediately above the knee, linch-pin, cf. gr. *ὠλένη*, lat. *ulna* and goth. *aleina*.

skr. *pāṇí-ṣ*, hand, cf. gr. *παλάμη*, lat. *palma*, ags. *folm*.

In loans from Prākrit dialects *ṇ* may represent the idg. combination *rn*:

skr. *gaṇá-s*, troop, cf. gr. *ἀγείρω*.

§ 73. **Skr. ṅ.** Skr. *ṅ* = idg. *n̄*:

skr. *aṅká-s*, lap, hook, gr. *ὄγκος*, lat. *uncus*.

skr. *bhaṅgá-s*, wave, cf. lith. *banga*.

§ 74. **Skr. ñ.** Before palatal affricates, which represent idg. velars or middle gutturals, skr. *ñ* goes back on idg. *n̄*. Before *j*, idg. *ĝ* the *ñ* is original.

Skr. *ñ* = idg. *n̄*:

skr. *páñca*, five, gr. *πέντε*, lat. *quinque*, goth. *fimf*.

§ 75. **Nasalization of vowels.** The nasalization of vowels is a remainder of idg. nasals. In Sanskrit all nasals before original or secondary spirants were reduced to anusvāra:

skr. *áṁsa-s*, shoulder, goth. *ams*, cf. gr. *ὦμος* and lat. *umerus*.

skr. *haṁsá-s*, goose, swan &c., cf. gr. *χήν*, ohg. *gans* and lat. *anser*.

skr. *ānáṁça*, perf. of *açnómi*, I attain, *áṁça-s*, portion, part, cf. gr. *ἤνεγκον*, lat. *nanciscor*.

ved. *áṁhas*, distress, lat. *angus-* in *angustus*, cf. gr. *ἄγχω*, lat. *angō* and goth. *aggwus*.

Liquids.

§ 76. **Skr. r.** Skr. *r* regularly corresponds to idg. *r*, but in many cases it goes back on idg. *l*.

Skr. *r* = idg. *r*:

skr. *rájyāmi*, I am (get) red, affected with a strong feeling, gr. *ῥέζω*.

skr. *rá-s*, riches, wealth, lat. *rēs*.

skr. *ráṭ* (**rāk* from **rākṣ*), king, lat. *rēx*.

skr. *bhárāmi*, I bear, gr. *φέρω*, lat. *ferō*, goth. *baíra*.

skr. *pári*, around, gr. πέρι, lat. *per*, goth. *faír-*.

skr. *smárāmi*, I remember, cf. lat. *memor*.

skr. voc. *mătar*, mother, gr. μῆτερ.

Skr. *r* = idg. *l*:

skr. *riréca*, I left, gr. λέλοιπα, goth. *laihw*.

skr. *rákṣāmi*, I protect, cf. gr. ἀλέξω.

ved. *rámbate*, hangs down, skr. *lámbate* (already Çat. Br.), cf. lat. *lābor*.

ved. *réhmi*, I lick, skr. *léhmi*, cf. gr. λείχω, lat. *lingō*, goth. *-laigōn*.

About the relation of the Vedic dialect to Sanskrit (the Brāhmaṇa's and the epic poems included) see § 43.

§ 77. **Skr. l.** Skr. *l* regularly corresponds to idg. *l*:

skr. *lámbate*, hangs down, cf. lat. *lābor*.

skr. *léhmi*, I lick, cf. gr. λείχω &c.

skr. *limpámi*, I smear, cf. gr. λίπος, λιπαρός &c.

skr. *lúbhyāmi*, I desire, cf. lat. *lubet*, goth. *liufs*.

skr. *álpa-s*, small, cf. lith. *alpnas*, weak.

But we often find skr. *l* = idg. *r* (cf. § 42):

skr. *luñcāmi*, I pull out, I pull off &c., cf. gr. ὀρύσσω, lat. *runcāre*.

skr. *lumpámi*, I break, cf. lat. *rumpō*, ags. *réofan*.

Labial explosives.

§ 78. **Skr. p.** Skr. *p* = idg. *p*:

skr. *purás*, in front &c., gr. πάρος, cf. goth. *faúra*.

skr. *paraçú-ṣ*, axe, gr. πέλεκυς, cf. goth. *filhan*.

skr. *pṛçni-ṣ*, speckled, cf. gr. περκνός and perhaps ohg. *forhana*.

skr. *parut*, last year, cf. gr. πέρυσι, mhg. *vĕrt*.

skr. *prá-*, forward, gr. πρό, goth. *fra-*, cf. lat. *prō(d)*.

skr. *plávāmi*, I float &c., gr. πλέω, cf. lat. *pluit* and ags. *fléotan*.

ved. *nápāt*, descendant, lat. *nepōs*, ohg. *nefo*.

skr. *sárpāmi*, I creep &c., gr. ἕρπω, lat. *serpō*.

§ 79. **Skr. ph.** Skr. *ph* = idg. *ph* (cf. § 46)?

skr. *phéna-s*, foam, cf. oslav. *péna* and ohg. *feim*.

skr. *phalgu-ṣ*, weak, worthless, useless, cf. gr. φελγύνει· ἀσυνετεῖ, ληρεῖ (Hesych.).

skr. *çaphá-s*, hoof, cf. ohg. *huof*.

§ 80. **Skr. b.** Skr. *b* = idg. *b*:

skr. *bála-m*, strength, power, cf. oslav. *bolij* and lat. *dēbilis*.

skr. *buk-kāra-s*, roar, bellow, cf. gr. βύκτης, βυκάνη, lat. *būcina*.

skr. *lámbate*, hangs down, cf. lat. *lābitur*.

ved. *upa-bdá-s*, stamping, trampling, cf. gr. ἐπίβδαι.

In the neighbourhood of a following aspirate *b* often represents idg. *bh*:

skr. *bódhāmi*, I perceive, goth. *biuda*, cf. gr. πεύθομαι, πυνθάνομαι.

ved. *budhná-s*, bottom, cf. gr. πυθμήν, πύνδαξ, lat. *fundus* and ohg. *bodam*.

In younger texts we often meet with dialectic words, in which *b* is written instead of *v*.

§ 81. **Skr. bh.** Skr. *bh* = idg. *bh*:

skr. *bhárāmi*, I bear, gr. φέρω, lat. *ferō*, goth. *baíra*.

skr. *bhávāmi*, I am, cf. gr. φύω, lat. *fui*, ohg. *būan*.

skr. *bhrû-ṣ*, eye-brow, cf. gr. ὀφρῦς and ohg. *brāwa*.

skr. *nábhas*, cloud, sky, gr. νέφος, cf. νεφέλη, lat. *nebula*, ohg. *nebul*.

skr. *jámbha-s*, set of teeth, tooth, gr. γόμφος, ohg. *chamb*.

Dental explosives.

§ 82. **Skr. t.** Skr. *t* = idg. *t*:

skr. *tanú-ṣ*, thin, gr. ταvu-, cf. lat. *tenuis*, ohg. *dunni*.

skr. *tudámi*, I push, I strike, cf. lat. *tundō* and goth. *stautan*.

skr. *tráyas*, three, gr. τρεῖς, lat. *trēs*, goth. *þreis*.

skr. *pátāmi*, I fly, I fall, lat. *petō*, cf. gr. πέτομαι, πίπτω.

skr. *kártāmi* (more common *kṛntámi*), I cut, lith. *kertu*.

skr. *pátnī*, lady, mistress, wife, cf. gr. πότνια·

In the combination *ts* the skr. *t* often goes back on idg. *s*:

skr. *vatsyámi*, I shall put on, gr. ἕσσω·

skr. *vidvátsu*, loc. plur. of *vidváṁs-*, knowing.

§ 83. **Skr. th.** Skr. *th* = idg. *th* (cf. § 49):

skr. *véttha*, thou knowest, gr. οἶσθα, cf. goth. *waist*.

In Sanskrit there are very few words beginning with *th*: these few partly have an onomatopoetic character and partly are borrowed from other dialects.

§ 84. **Skr. d.** Skr. *d* = idg. *d*:

skr. *dádāmi*, I give, gr. δίδωμι, cf. lat. *dō*.

skr. *dáça*, ten, gr. δέκα, lat. *decem*, goth. *taíhun*.

skr. *dváu*, ved. *dvá*, two, gr. δύω, lat. *duō*, cf. goth. pl. *twai*.

skr. *ádmi*, I eat, cf. gr. ἔδω, lat. *edō*, goth. *ita*.

skr. *chinádmi*, I cut off, cf. gr. σχίζω, σχινδαλμός, lat. *scindō*.

Before *bh* the skr. *d* sometimes goes back on idg. *z*:

ved. *mādbhíṣ*, instr. pl. of *más*, moon, month.

Skr. *ed* in some cases represents ar. *azd* (see § 63):

ved. *sedyát*, 3 pers. sing. optat. perf. of *sad-*, to sit, avest. *hazdyāþ*.

In the neighbourhood of a following aspirate *d* often goes back on idg. *dh*:

skr. *dádhāmi*, I put, gr. τίθημι.

§ 85. **Skr. dh.** Skr. *dh* = idg. *dh*:

skr. *dhárṣāmi*, I dare, cf. gr. θρασύς, θαρρέω, goth. *ga-dars*.

skr. *dhūmá-s*, smoke, vapor, gr. θῦμός, lat. *fūmus*.

skr. *dháyāmi*, I suck, I drink, goth. *daddja*, cf. gr. θῆσθαι, lat. *fēlāre*, *fēmina*.

skr. *mádhu*, honey, gr. μέθυ, ohg. *meto*.

skr. *mádhya-s*, middle, gr. μέσος, lat. *medius*, goth. *midjis*.

In the combinations *bdh, ddh, gdh* the skr. *dh* often goes back on an original *t*:

ved. *dábdhum*, to hurt: *dabhnómi*, I hurt.

ved. *baddhá-s*, bound: *badhnámi*, I bind.

skr. *dágdhum*, to burn: *dáhāmi*, I burn.

Skr. *edh* sometimes represents ar. *azdh* (see § 63):

skr. *edhí*, imper. of *as-*, to be, cf. avest. *zdī* and gr. ἴσθι.

Lingual explosives.

§ 86. **Skr. ṭ.** Skr. *ṭ* may correspond to idg. *t* (after *ṣ* and in prācritisms), to idg. *lt* and in loans from Prākrit dialects to idg. *rt*.

Skr. *ṭ* (after *ṣ*) = idg. *t*:

skr. *aṣṭáu*, ved. *aṣṭá*, eight, gr. ὀκτώ, lat. *octō*, goth. *ahtau*.

skr. *uṣṭá-s*, burned, lat. *ustus*.

Skr. *ṭ* (in prācritisms) = idg. *t*:

skr. *aṭāmi*, I roam, I wander about, ved. *átāmi*.

skr. *caṭāmi*, I hide myself, ved. *cátāmi*.

Skr. *ṭ* = idg. *lt*:

skr. *paṭa-s*, woven stuff, cloth, garment, cf. oslav. *platĭno*, russ. *polotnó*, linen.

skr. *páṭu-ṣ*, sharp, cf. gr. πλατύς, saltish.

skr. *spháṭāmi*, I burst, cf. ohg. *spaltan*.

Skr. *ṭ* (in prācritisms) = idg. *rt*:

skr. *bhaṭa-s*, soldier: *bhṛtá-s*, hired (cf. gr. φέρω).

skr. *káṭa-s*, mat: *kartana-m*, spinning (cf. gr. κύρτος, κάρ-
ταλος, lat. *crātēs*, goth. *haúrds*).

skr. *kaṭú-ṣ*, sharp: *kart-*, to cut (cf. lith. *kartus*).

The *ṭ* in the nom. sing. and loc. pl. of the stems ending
in *ç, j, ṣ* is to be explained by analogy:

skr. *víṭ*, clan, people, nom. of *viç-*, cf. *veça-s*, house, gr.
οῖκος, lat. *vicus* and goth. *weihs*. The regular nominative of
viç- would have been **vik* (from **vikṣ*, idg. **u̯iḱ-s*).

skr. *ráṭ*, king, nom. of *rāj-*, cf. lat. *rēx*, gen. *rēgis*. Here
also might have been expected a nominative ending in *k*,
viz. **rāk* (from **rākṣ*, idg. **rēḱ-s*).

skr. *dviṭ*, hating, nom. of *dviṣ-*. The regular nominative
would have been **dvik* (from **dvikṣ*, idg. **du̯is-s*).

In the *bh*-cases of these stems *ḍ* was regular: *viḍbhíṣ* from
idg. **u̯iǵbhis*, *rāḍbhíṣ* from idg. **rēǵbhis*, *dviḍbhíṣ* from idg.
**du̯izbhis*, see § 60 and § 63. These cases made it possible,
that a locat. pl. and a nom. sing. with *ṭ* were formed.

§ 87. **Skr. ṭh.** Skr. *ṭh* = idg. *lth*:

skr. *jaṭhara-m*, belly, womb, cf. goth. *kilþei*.

skr. *kuṭhāra-s*, axe, lat. *culter*.

In prācritisms *ṭh* sometimes occurs instead of *th*. At the
beginning of words *ṭh* is very rare.

§ 88. **Skr. ḍ.** Skr. *ḍ* may represent idg. *ld, zd, z, ǵ* and
in prācritisms idg. *d* and *rd*.

Skr. *ḍ* = idg. *ld*:

skr. *jaḍa-s*, cold &c., cf. lat. *gelu*, *gelāre*, icel. *kala* &c. (?).

Skr. *ḍ* = idg. *zd* (after *ĭ, ŭ, i̯, u̯*):

skr. *niḍá-s*, nest, lat. *nīdus*, ohg. *nest*.

Skr. *ḍ* = idg. *z* (after *ĭ, ŭ, i̯, u̯* before *bh*):

skr. *dviḍbhíṣ*, instr. pl. of *dviṣ-*, hating.

Skr. *ḍ* = idg. *ĝ* (before *bh*):

skr. *viḍbhíṣ*, instr. pl. of *viç-*, clan, people.

§ 89. **Skr. ḍh.** Skr. *ḍh* may represent idg. *ldh, zdh, ĝh + t* and in prācritisms idg. *rdh* and *dh*.

Skr. *ḍh* = idg. *ldh*: no certain example.

Skr. *ḍh* = idg. *zdh* (after *ĭ, ŭ, i̥, u̥*):

ved. *ástoḍhvam*, 2 pers. pl. aor. med. of *stáumi*, I praise.

Skr. *ḍh* = idg. *ĝh + t*:

skr. *léḍhi*, licks: *léhmi*, I lick.

skr. *dṛḍhá-s*, firm: *dṛ́hyāmi*, I make firm.

skr. *vóḍhum*, to carry, *váhāmi*, I carry.

Guttural explosives.

§ 90. **Skr. k.** In general skr. *k* represents the idg. *q* and *k*.

Skr. *k* = idg. *q*:

skr. *kásate*, coughs, cf. ags. *hwósta*.

skr. *katará-s*, who (from two), gr. πότερος, goth. *hwapar*.

skr. *yákṛt*, liver, cf. gr. ἥπαρ, lat. *jecur*.

skr. *paṅktí-ṣ*, row of five, row, cf. gr. πέμπτος.

Skr. *k* = idg. *k*:

skr. *kakút* (*d*), summit, cf. lat. *cacūmen*.

skr. *karká-s*, crab, cf. gr. καρκίνος, lat. *cancer*.

ved. *kravíṣ*, raw flesh, gr. κρέας, cf. lat. *cruor*.

The combination *kṣ* may go back on different consonant-groups.

Skr. *kṣ* = idg. *ks* (*qs*):

skr. *dhakṣyámi*, I shall burn, lith. *deksiu*, cf. skr. *dáhāmi*, I burn, lith. *degu* (also skr. *ni-dāghá-*, heat, summer, opruss. *dagis*, summer, goth. *dags* &c.).

skr. *vákṣi*, 2 pers. of *vácmi*, I say, cf. *vácas*, word, *vák*, voice, gr. *ἔπος*, *ὄπ-*, lat. *vōx* &c.

skr. *vakṣyámi*, fut. of *vácmi*, I say.

skr. *úkṣāmi*, I grow, perf. *vavákṣa*, cf. gr. *ἀέξω*, goth. *wahsjan* &c. Lith. *auksztas*, high, proves, that we have to do with idg. *ks*.

Skr. *kṣ* = idg. *k̂s*:

skr. *vákṣi*, 2 pers. of *váçmi*, I will, cf. gr. *ἐκών*.

skr. *ákṣa-s*, axle, cf. gr. *ἄξων*, lat. *axis*, ohg. *ahsa*, lith. *aszis*, oslav. *osĭ*.

skr. *dákṣiṇa-s*, right, southern, avest. *dašina-*, oslav. *desĭnŭ*, lith. fem. *deszinė*, cf. gr. *δεξιός*, lat. *dexter*, goth. *taíhswa*.

Skr. *kṣ* = idg. *ss* (after *ĭ*, *ŭ*, *i̯*, *u̯*):

skr. *dvékṣi*, 2 pers. of *dvéṣmi*, I hate.

skr. *çokṣyámi*, I shall dry up, gr. *αὕσω*.

Skr. *kṣ* = guttural + *p* (*d̶*): see § 67.

§ 91. **Skr. kh.** Skr. *kh* = idg. *kh* (*gh*):

skr. *çaṅkhá-s*, shell, gr. *κόγχος*.

skr. *skhálāmi*, I stumble, cf. gr. *σφάλλω*?

§ 92. **Skr. g.** Skr. *g* corresponds to idg. *g̑*, *g*.

Skr. *g* = idg. *g̑*:

skr. *gáu-ṣ*, bull, cow, gr. *βοῦς*, lat. **vōs* (*bōs*), ohg. *chuo*.

skr. *gurú-ṣ*, heavy, cf. gr. *βαρύς*, goth. *kaúrus* (also lat. *gravis*).

skr. *ágāt*, went, gr. *ἔβη*.

Skr. *g* = idg. *g*:

skr. *yugá-m*, yoke, age, gr. *ζυγόν*, lat. *jugum*, goth. *juk*.

skr. *ugrá-s*, mighty, terrible, cf. lat. *augeō*, goth. *aukan*.

In the neighbourhood of a following aspirate we often find *g* from *g̑h* or *gh*:

skr. *gŕdhyāmi*, I am eager, cf. goth. *grēdus*.

§ 93. **Skr. gh.** Skr. *gh* goes back on idg. *g̑h* or *gh*.

Skr. *gh* = idg. *g̑h*:

skr. *ghaná-s*, slayer (ved.), compact &c., gr. φόνος, cf. ohg. *gundea*, ags. *gúð*.

Skr. *gh* = idg. *gh*:

skr. *dīrghá-s*, long, cf. gr. δολιχός.

Palatal affricates.

§ 94. **Skr. c.** Skr. *c* in general represents idg. *q*, *k* before palatal vowels and *i̯*.

Skr. *c* = idg. *q*:

skr. *carú-ṣ*, pot, kettle, icel. *hverr*.

skr. *catvắraṣ*, four, goth. *fidwŏr*, cf. gr. τέσσαρες, lat. *quatuor*.

skr. *páñca*, five, gr. πέντε, lat. *quinque*, goth. *fimf*.

Skr. *c* = idg. *k*:

skr. *cyávate*, moves, falls, cf. gr. σεύω.

skr. *rócate*, shines, pleases, cf. gr. λευκός, lat. *lūx*, *lūcet*, goth. *liuhaþ*.

In cases as *ucca-*, high, the first *c* is an assimilated *t* (here originally *d*).

§ 95. **Skr. ch.** On the origin of skr. *ch* see § 55. Instances:

skr. *chinádmi*, I cut off, cf. avest. *sid-*, gr. σχίζω, lat. *scindō*.

skr. *gácchati*, goes, cf. avest. *jasaiti*, gr. βάσκω.

§ 96. **Skr. j.** Skr. *j* represents the idg. *g̑*, *g*, before palatal vowels and *i̯*, as well as the idg. *ĝ*.

Skr. *j* = idg. *g̑*:

ved. *járate*, crackles, invokes, cf. ohg. *quirit*.

Skr. *j* = idg. *g*:

skr. *ójas*, strength, power, cf. *ugrá-s*, mighty, terrible, lat. *augeō* and goth. *aukan*.

Skr. *j* = idg. *ĝ*:

ved. *jánas*, race, family, gr. *γένος*, lat. *genus*, cf. goth. *kuni*.

skr. *jánu*, knee, cf. gr. *γόνυ*, lat. *genu*, goth. *kniu*.

skr. *juṣámi*, I take pleasure, I relish, cf. gr. *γεύω*, goth. *kiusa* and lat. *gustus*, goth. *kustus*.

skr. *bhūrja-s*, birch, cf. ohg. *pirihha*.

skr. *mṛjámi*, I rub, wipe, strip, cf. gr. *ἀμέλγω*, lat. *mulgeō*, ohg. *milchu*.

In cases as ved. *újjiti-ṣ*, victory, the first *j* is an assimilated *d*.

In the neighbourhood of a following aspirate *j* may represent the idg. aspirates *ǵh*, *gh*, *ĝh*:

skr. *jagráha*, seized: *gṛhṇámi*.

skr. *jáhāti*, leaves, avest. *zazāiti*.

§ 97. **Skr. jh.** In skr. *ujjhitá-s*, left, from *ud* + **jhitá-s*, the skr. *jh* goes back on idg. *ĝh*: cf. *jáhāmi*, I leave. Most words containing *jh* are not clear.

Spirants.

§ 98. **Skr. ç.** In general skr. *ç* corresponds to idg. *ḱ*, but in some cases it is an assimilated *s*.

Skr. *ç* = idg. *ḱ*:

skr. *çatá-m*, hundred, gr. *ἑ-κατόν*, lat. *centum*, goth. *hund*.

skr. *çankú-ṣ*, wedge, oslav. *sǫkŭ*, branch.

skr. *çáṁsāmi*, I praise, I recite &c., cf. lat. *censeō*.

skr. *veça-s*, house, gr. *οἶκος*, lat. *vicus*, cf. goth. *weihs*.

skr. *dáçāmi*, I bite, cf. gr. *δάκνω*.

ved. *áçmā* (*n*), stone, gr. *ἄκμων*.

skr. *dadárça*, I have seen, gr. *δέδορκα*.

Skr. *ç* = idg. *s*:

skr. *çváçura-s*, father in law, gr. ἐκυρός, cf. lat. *socer* and goth. *swaíhra*.

skr. *çaçá-s*, hare, cf. ohg. *haso*.

§ 99. **Skr. ṣ.** Skr. *ṣ* lingualized from idg. *s*:

skr. *tíṣṭhāmi*, I stand, gr. ἵστημι.

skr. *uṣṭá-s*, burned, lat. *ustus*.

skr. *vṛkeṣu*, loc. pl. of *vṛka-s*, wolf, cf. oslav. *vlŭcěchŭ*.

ved. *joṣṭar-*, loving, cf. gr. γευστήριον.

skr. *dvékṣi*, 2 pers. of *dvéṣmi*, I hate.

skr. *dhṛṣṇómi*, *dhárṣāmi*, I dare, cf. gr. θαρρέω and goth. *gadars*.

In the combination *ṣṭ* the skr. *ṣ* often represents idg. *k̂*:

skr. *aṣṭá* (ved.), *aṣṭáu*, eight, gr. ὀκτώ, lat. *octō*, goth. *ahtau*.

skr. *diṣṭi-ṣ*, indication &c., cf. ohg. *inziht*, lat. *dictiō*, gr. δεῖξις.

How the *ṣ* of *ṣaṭ*, six, is to be explained, is yet uncertain: probably an initial consonant has been lost, cf. avest. χṣ́vaš́.

Skr. *ṣ* = idg. *p*, *đ*: see § 67.

§ 100. **Skr. s.** Skr. *s* = idg. *s*:

skr. *saptá*, seven, gr. ἑπτά, lat. *septem*, cf. goth. *sibun*.

ved. *sána-s*, old, gr. fem. ἕνη, cf. lat. *senex* and goth. *sineigs*.

skr. *sáhas*, strength, might, violence, goth. *sigis*.

skr. *svásā* (*r*), sister, lat. *soror*, goth. *swistar*.

skr. *srávāmi*, I flow, I stream, gr. ῥέω, cf. ohg. *stroum*.

skr. *váste*, clothes one's self, puts on, cf. gr. ἕννῡμι, ἐσθής, lat. *vestis*, goth. *wasjan*.

§ 101. **Skr. h.** Skr. *h* may go back on idg. *g̑h*, *gh* before palatal vowels and *i̯*, further on idg. *ĝh* and in dialectic words and forms on idg. *bh* and *đh*.

Skr. *h* = idg. *g̑h*:

skr. *hánmi*, I slay, cf. gr. θείνω and skr. *hatyā*, slaughter, ohg. *gundea*, ags. *gúđ*.

ved. *háras*, heat, gr. θέρος.

Skr. *h* = idg. *gh*:

ved. *drúhas*, harming spirits, cf. *drúhyāmi*, I harm, ohg. *triogan*.

Skr. *h* = idg. *ǧh*:

ved. *héman-*, winter, gr. χεῖμα, χειμών, cf. gr. χιών, lat. *hiems* &c.

skr. *haṁsá-s*, goose, swan &c., cf. gr. χήν, lat. *anser*, ohg. *gans*.

skr. *bāhú-ṣ*, arm, gr. πῆχυς, ohg. *buog*.

skr. *léhmi*, I lick, cf. gr. λείχω, lat. *lingō*, goth. *-laigōn*.

Skr. *h* = idg. *bh*:

skr. *hárāmi*, I bear, I take, cf. *bhárāmi*, I bear, gr. φέρω &c.

skr. *gṛhṇā́mi*, I seize, cf. ved. *gṛbhṇā́mi*.

Skr. *h* = idg. *dh*:

Skr. *-hi*, suffix of the 2 pers. sing. imperat. act., cf. *-dhi*, gr. -θι.

skr. *-mahe, -mahi*, suffixes of the 1 pers. pl. med., gr. -μεθα.

In some words the skr. *h* seems to correspond to gr. γ, goth. *k*: see § 66.

PART III.

SANDHI-SYSTEM.

§ 102. **General remarks**. The rules, which govern the changes of the initial and final sounds of words in the sentence and in composition, are called *sandhi*-rules. Of course already in the mother-language the final sounds of preceding words and the initial sounds of following words had a mutual influence on each other, but it is impossible to reconstruct a complete tableau of this Indogermanic sandhi. Yet there are reasons to suppose, that already in the Indogermanic period the explosives and spirants were voiced or voiceless according to their position before voiced or voiceless explosives and spirants. The double forms gr. $\pi\rho o\tau i$ = skr. *práti* and gr. $\pi\rho ó\varsigma$ = skr. *práty* may prove, that in the mother-language *i* before sonants became a semivowel, which suggests the supposition, that this was also the case with *u*. The simultaneous existence of the Indian dual-endings -*āu* = goth. -*au* (in *ahtau*) and -*ā* = gr. -*ω* allows the conclusion, that yet in a time of dialectic continuity the idg. diphthong -*ōu̯* before certain consonants or groups of consonants was simplified to -*ō*. Gr. $\H{\alpha}\kappa\mu\omega\nu$ and skr. *áçmā*, gr. $\pi\alpha\tau\H{\eta}\rho$ and skr. *pitá* stand in a similar relation to each other. By the side of roots beginning with *s* we often find doublets without that initial consonant (skr. *sthágāmi* : lat. *tegō*, goth. *stautan* : skr. *tudǎmi*) and hence we may conclude, that before the end of the Indogermanic period the initial *s* was lost, when preceded by a word ending in *s*. About these and other phenomena, which are explained by Indogermanic sandhi, see Brugmann 1, 490 sqq.

The Indian sandhi has gradually developed itself from that of the mother-language, because of which only a historical treatment of the sandhi-rules may claim a scientific value, but the uncertainty, which till now prevails in the history of the initial and final sounds, makes it preferable to arrange them systematically.

§ 103. **Final and initial vowels.** It is a rule in composition as well as in the sentence, that -*ǎ* + *ǎ*- are contracted to *ā*, -*ǐ* + *ǐ*- to *i*, -*ǔ* + *ǔ*- to *ū*. An *a*-vowel (-*ǎ*) combines with an *i*-vowel (*ǐ*-) to *e*, with an *u*-vowel (*ǔ*-) to *o*, with *r̥*- to *ar*, with *e*- and *āi*- to *āi*, with *o*- and *āu*- to *āu*, but -*ǐ*, -*ǔ* and -*r̥* before a dissimilar vowel or diphthong are changed each to its corresponding consonant (*y*, *v*, *r*). The original, but contracted diphthongs -*e* and -*o* remain unchanged before *a*-, which however disappears; before all other vowels they become *a* (we seldom find -*ay* and -*av*, which of course are the regular representatives of the antevocalic ar. -*ai̯* and -*au̯*: see § 7). The diphthongs -*āi* and -*āu* before all vowels may be retained unchanged (if so, they are written -*āy*, -*āv*), but it is also permitted to change them to -*ā*.

About some liberty in Sanskrit as to the treatment of final and initial vowels see Whitney § 127 *a*, § 129 *c*, § 133 *a*, § 134 *c* and cf. Kern, Taal en letteren 6, 332. The peculiarities of the Vedic vowelsandhi are noticed in Whitney's grammar, to which it will suffice to refer.

Contraction of similar vowels:

na + *asti* = *nāsti*, not is.

tatra + *āyātaḥ* = *tatrāyātaḥ*, there arrived.

gatvā + *abravīt* = *gatvābravīt*, having gone he (she) said.

rājā + *ādadāt* = *rājādadāt*, the king took.

asti + *iha* = *astiha*, is here.

adhi + *içvaraḥ* = *adhīçvaraḥ*, over-lord.

devī + *iyam* = *devīyam*, this goddess.

strī + *īkṣate* = *strīkṣate*, the woman sees.

su + *uktam* = *sūktam*, hymn.

bāhu- + *ūru-* = *bāhūru-*, arms and thighs.

Combination of ă with dissimilar vowels:

tiṣṭha + *iha* = *tiṣṭheha*, remain here.

ratha- + *īṣā* = *ratheṣā*, shaft of a chariot.

bhāryā + *iva* = *bhāryeva*, as a wife.

kā + *īdṛçī* = *kedṛçī*, who (fem.) is such a one.

huta- + *ucchiṣṭam* = *hutocchiṣṭam*, remains of a sacrifice.

vṛka- + *udara-* = *vṛkodara-*, who has a wolf's belly (epithet of Bhīma).

sahasā + *utthāya* = *sahasotthāya*, hastily arisen.

rambhā- + *ūru-* = *rambhoru-*, who has thighs as a banana.

sapta + *ṛṣayaḥ* = *saptarṣayaḥ*, the seven sages, the seven stars of the Great Bear.

mahā- + *ṛṣabhaḥ* = *maharṣabhaḥ*, a great (large) bull.

eka- + *ekaḥ* = *ekāikaḥ*, each.

mā + *evam* = *māivam*, not so (prohibitively).

jala- + *okas-* = *jalāukas-*, whose dwelling-place is the water, aquatic animal, leech.

mahā- + *oṣadhiḥ* = *mahāuṣadhiḥ*, a great simple.

loka- + *āiçvaryam* = *lokāiçvaryam*, dominion of the world.

mahā- + *āiçvaryam* = *mahāiçvaryam*, great dominion.

rūpa- + *āudārya-* = *rūpāudārya-*, beauty and generosity.

yathā + *āucityam* = *yathāucityam*, properly (according to custom).

Change of *ĭ*, *ŭ*, *ṛ* to *y*, *v*, *r* before dissimilar vowels:

iti + *uktvā* = *ityuktvā*, having spoken thus.

kuṭṭanī + *āha* = *kuṭṭanyāha*, the procuress said.

madhu + *iva* = *madhviva*, as honey.

pitṛ- + *artham* = *pitrartham*, for the father's sake.

Treatment of *e* and *o* before vowels:

tathāgate + *api* = *tathāgate'pi*, even under such circumstances, nevertheless.

bhāno + *atra* = *bhāno'tra*, sun (vocat.), here.

te + *āgatāḥ* = *ta āgatāḥ*, they have arrived.

nagare + *iha* = *nagara iha*, here in the town.

sūno + *ehi* = *sūna(v) ehi*, son (vocat.), come.

Treatment of *āi*, *āu* before vowels:

tasmāi + *adadāt* = *tasmā(y) adadāt*, he (she) gave him.

tāu + *ūcatuḥ* = *tā(v) ūcatuḥ*, those two said.

Certain final vowels maintain themselves unchanged before any following vowel (Whitney § 138):

1° the vowels *ī*, *ū* and *e* as dual endings, both in nominal and in verbal forms;

2° the pronoun *amī* (nom. pl.), those;

3° the vowels of interjections as *aho*, *he* &c.

Some other exceptions to the vowel-sandhi are of less importance.

§ 104. **Simplification of consonant-groups.** The final *s* (*ṣ*) and *t* disappeared, when preceded by one or more consonants. If there remained after the dropping of *s* (*ṣ*) or *t* an other combination than *r* + explosive, even that was simplified. About probable traces of postconsonantic *t* and *s* see § 105.

Dropping of postconsonantic *s* (*ṣ*):

vāk from **vāk-ṣ*, voice, cf. avest. *vāχš*, lat. *vōx*.

adhok from **adhok-ṣ*, 2 pers. sing. impf. of *dohmi*, I milk.

pāt from **pāt-s*, foot, cf. gr. dor. πώς.

açāt from **açāt-s*, older **açās-s*, 2 pers. sing. impf. of *çāsmi*, I rule &c.: see § 62. The form *açāt* as 2 pers. does not seem to occur in literature, but is warranted by its *ts* from *ss*. The 3 pers. is also *açāt*, but here the *t* is not regular: **açās-t* would have given **açās*. It is not surprising, that the organic paradigm *açāsam*, *açāt*, *açās* has been changed by analogy to *açāsam*, *açās*, *açāt*.

ajāiṣ (*ajāiḥ*, see § 109) from **ajāiṣṭ*, 3 pers. sing. aor. of *jayāmi*, I conquer.

ahan from **ahan-s*, 2 pers. sing. impf. of *hanmi*, I slay.

vṛkān, agnin, paraçūn from **vṛkăns*, **agnĭns*, **paraçŭns*, acc. pl. of *vṛka-s*, wolf, *agni-ṣ*, fire, *paraçu-ṣ*, axe, cf. goth. *dagans, anstins, sununs*, gr. cret. λύκονς, τρίνς, υἰὐνς &c.

akar from **akar-ṣ*, 2 pers. sing. aor. of *karomi*, I make.

Dropping of postconsonantic *t*:

adhok from **adhok-t*, 3 pers. sing. impf. of *dohmi*, I milk.

ahan from **ahan-t*, 3 pers. sing. impf. of *hanmi*, I slay.

akar from **akar-t*, 3 pers. sing. aor. of *karomi*, I make.

Dropping of two or more consonants:

prāṅ from **prāṅk-ṣ*, eastern.

bharan from **bharant-s*, bearing, cf. goth. *baírands*.

achān from **achănts-t*, 3 pers. sing. aor. (1 pers. *achăntsam*) of *chand-*, to appear, to please.

Examples of *r* + explosive remaining unchanged after the loss of a final *s* (*ṣ*):

ūrk from **ūrk-ṣ*, strength, vigor.

suhārt from **suhārt-s*, having a good heart.

In cases as *viṭ*, *dviṭ* &c. the *ṭ* is not organic: see § 86.

§ 105. **Final nasals.** In general it is a rule, that final nasals, as to the place of their articulation, are assimilated to a following consonant, but before labials and gutturals -*n* is not modified.

The -*n*, -*ñ* (from -*n*), -*ṇ* (from -*n*) before a following *t*- (*th*-), *c*- (*ch*-), *ṭ* (*ṭh*-) usually insert a sibilant: its mode of articulation depends on the following initial consonant. Before the inserted sibilant the nasal becomes anusvāra. The origin of this rule is probably due to the circumstance, that the idg. -*ns* was simplified to -*n* (see § 104), except before those voiceless dentals, palatal affricates and linguals.

The combination of -*n* + *ç*- is -*ñ ç*- as well as -*ñ ch*-. In the same way -*n* + *s*- and -*n* + *ṣ*- are often combined to -*nt s*-, -*nt ṣ*-.

The -*n* before *l*- is assimilated to -*l*, after nasalizing the preceding vowel. The labial nasal -*m* before *y*-, *v*-, *r*-, *l*-, *h*- and sibilants becomes anusvāra.

All nasals except -*m*, when preceded by a short vowel, are doubled before any initial vowel.

Partial assimilation of nasals to initial consonants:

tam + *daridram* = *tan daridram*, that poor man (acc.).

apaçyam + *ḍākinīm* = *apaçyaṇ ḍākinim*, I saw a witch.

imam + *kumāram* = *imaṅ kumāram*, this boy (acc.)

pāṇim + *jagrāha* = *pāṇiñ jagrāha*, I (he) seized the hand.

pakṣin + *ḍayase* = *pakṣiṇ ḍayase*, bird (voc.), thou art flying.

tān + *janān* = *tāñ janān*, those people (acc.).

Examples of -*n* before voiceless dentals, palatal affricates and linguals:

tān + *tarūn* = *tāṁs tarūn*, those trees (acc.).

tān + *cārān* = *tāṁç cārān*, those spies (acc.).

tān + *ṭaṅkān* = *tāṁṣ ṭaṅkān*, those pickaxes (acc.)

In many cases this *s* (*ç*, *ṣ*) has an etymological value: *tān* goes back on idg. **tons* (gr. cret. τόνς, goth. *þans*) and so *tāṁs tarūn* regularly represents an original **tons tèruns*.

Examples of *-n* before sibilants:

tān + *çatrūn* = *tāñ çatrūn* or *tāñ chatrūn*, those enemies (acc.).

mahān + *san* = *mahān san* or *mahānt san*, being great.

tān + *ṣaṭ* = *tān ṣaṭ* or *tānt ṣaṭ*, those six (acc.)

Example of *-n* + *l-*:

tān + *lokān* = *tāṁl lokān*, those worlds (acc.).

Examples of *-m* before semivowels, liquids, *h-* and sibilants:

tām + *yātrām* = *tāṁ yātrām*, that festive train (acc.).

gahanam + *vanam* = *gahanaṁ vanam*, a thick forest.

bahumūlyam + *ratnam* = *bahumūlyaṁ ratnam*, a precious jewel.

tam + *laguḍam* = *taṁ laguḍam*, that cudgel (acc.).

vṛkam + *hanmi* = *vṛkaṁ hanmi*, I slay a wolf.

jalam + *sravati* = *jalaṁ sravati*, the water flows.

vīrāṇām + *çauryam* = *vīrāṇāṁ çauryam*, the valor of heroes.

çoṇitam + *ṣṭhivati* = *çoṇitaṁ ṣṭhivati*, he (she) spits blood.

Gemination of nasals after a short vowel:

gacchan + *apatat* = *gacchann apatat*, going, he fell.

pratyaṅ + *āsīnaḥ* = *pratyaṅṅ āsīnaḥ*, sitting towards the west.

But:

annam + *icchati* = *annam icchati*, he (she) desires food.

§ 106. **Voiced and voiceless explosives.** In general Sanskrit has maintained the Indogermanic rules. Voiced explosives become voiceless before voiceless consonants and in pausa; voiceless explosives become voiced before voiced consonants and (a specific Sanskrit phenomenon) before vowels. The change of tenues to mediae before vowels is to be explained by analogy: see Brugmann 1, 494.

Change of mediae to tenues before voiceless consonants and in pausa:

tad + *phalam* = *tat phalam*, that fruit.

tasmād + *samudrād* = *tasmāt samudrāt*, from that ocean.

Change of tenues to mediae before voiced consonants and vowels:

ṛtvik + *bhāṣate* = *ṛtvig bhāṣate*, the priest speaks.

avasat + *vārāṇasyām* = *avasad vārāṇasyām*, he (she) dwelt in Benares.

akriṇāt + *annam* = *akriṇād annam*, he (she) bought food.

§ 107. **Explosives before nasals.** Final explosives, when followed by an initial nasal, are converted to their homorganic nasals. Only the assimilation of -*d* to -*n* is in harmony with the general phonetic rules of Sanskrit (see § 50).

Examples:

vāk + *mama* = *vāṅ mama*, my voice.

viḍ- + *mūtra-* = *viṇmūtra-*, faeces and urine (the *ṇ* is to be explained by assuming, that from the *bh-* cases of *viṣ-* a stem *viḍ-* was abstracted, which afterwards was composed with *mūtra-*. The nom. *viṭ* is a similar analogous formation).

tad + *nagaram* = *tan nagaram*, that town.

§ 108. **Assimilation of dental explosives to palatal affricates, to ç, to linguals and to l.** The dental explosives are totally assimilated to the initial consonant of the following word, if this consonant is a nasal (see § 107), a palatal affricate, a lingual or a *l*. With an initial *ç-* the dental explosives are combined to *cch*.

Examples:

tad + *ca* = *tac ca*, and that.

bhavat- + *jāmātā* = *bhavajjāmātā*, your son in law.

atāḍayat + *ḍiṇḍimam* = *atāḍayaḍ ḍiṇḍimam*, he beat the drum.

tad + *loham* = *tal loham*, that iron.

tad + *çṛṇomi* = *tac chṛṇomi*, I hear that.

§ 109. **Treatment of -s and -ṣ.** Only after the Aryan *a* and *ā* the *-s* was preserved unchanged, after *ĭ, ŭ* and diphthongs it had become *-š* before the end of the Aryan period. In Indian this *-š* was lingualized (*-ṣ*). About *-s* (*-ṣ*) after consonants see § 104. The sandhi-rules concerning *-s* and *-ṣ* may be formulated as follows:

Before *t-* (*th-*) the original *-s* remains unchanged, but *-ṣ* is converted to *-s*; before *ṭ-* (*ṭh-*) the *-ṣ* remains unchanged, but *-s* becomes *-ṣ*; before *c-* (*ch-*) the dental and the lingual sibilants are both palatalized, i. e. converted to *-ç*. As to the conversion of *-ṣ* to *-s* before dentals (*t-, th-*) it is to be remarked, that in the Veda often occur cases as *agníṣ ṭvā*, *çúciṣ ṭvám*, in which the assimilation has followed an opposite direction: here the final *-ṣ* has assimilated the initial dental (*agníṣ*, fire, + *tvā*, thee; *çúciṣ*, clear, pure, + *tvám*, thou), which is in harmony with the treatment of *ṣ* + *t* in internal combination (see § 49). Before *k* (*kh*), *p* (*ph*) and in pausa *-s* and *-ṣ* become visarga: yet in the Veda cases as *vástoṣ pátiḥ*, *ā́yuṣ kṛṇotu* are not rare (*vástoṣ*, gen. of *vástu-*, house, + *pátiḥ*, lord; *ā́yuṣ*, long life, + *kṛṇotu*, may he make). Before sibilants *-s* and *-ṣ* are either assimilated or converted to visarga. Before voiced consonants, except *r-*, and before vowels *-ṣ* becomes *-r*, but before *r-* the *-ṣ* disappears after lengthening a preceding *i* or *u*. Before voiced consonants and before *a-* the very common ending *-as* becomes *-o*, but before other vowels it becomes *-a*; in *-ās* the *-s* is dropped before voiced consonants as well as before vowels without leaving any trace. After the *-o*, which goes back on *-as*, an initial *a-* disappears. On the probable course of development of this system see Brugmann 1, 495.

The unchanged -*s* before *t*-:

nṛpas + *tuṣyati* = *nṛpas tuṣyati*, the king is satisfied (pleased).

namas tasmāi = *namas tasmāi*, reverence to him.

Dentalization of -*ṣ* before *t*-:

agniṣ + *tiṣṭhati* = *agnis tiṣṭhati*, a fire stands.

guruṣ + *tāḍayati* = *gurus tāḍayati*, the teacher beats.

The unchanged -*ṣ* before *ṭ*-:

paraçuṣ + *ṭaṅkaç ca* = *paraçuṣ ṭaṅkaç ca*, hatchet and pickaxe.

Lingualization of -*s* before *ṭ*-:

ṭiṭṭibhas + *ṭiṭṭibhī ca* = *ṭiṭṭibhaṣ ṭiṭṭibhī ca*, male and female of Parra jacana.

Palatalization of -*s* and -*ṣ* before *c*- (*ch*-):

kumbhilas + *corayati* = *kumbhilaç corayati*, the thief steals.

çatruṣ + *chinatti* = *çatruç chinatti*, the foe cuts off.

Change of -*s* and -*ṣ* to visarga before *k*-, *kh*-, *p*-, *ph*-:

amātyas + *kupyati* = *amātyaḥ kupyati*, the minister is angry.

taruṣ + *kampate* = *taruḥ kampate*, the tree is trembling, being shaken.

naras + *khādati* = *naraḥ khādati*, the man eats.

paçuṣ + *khidyate* = *paçuḥ khidyate*, the animal is being teased.

khecarās + *patanti* = *khecarāḥ patanti*, the birds fly.

mṛtyoṣ + *pāças* = *mṛtyoḥ pāçaḥ*, the bond of death.

apaçyas + *phalāni* = *apaçyaḥ phalāni*, thou sawest fruits.

Change of -*s* and -*ṣ* to visarga in pausa:

yudhyante + *kṣatriyās* = *yudhyante kṣatriyāḥ*, the noblemen fight.

rakṣati + *nṛpas* = *rakṣati nṛpaḥ*, the king protects.

çūdrāṇām + *jātis* = *çūdrānāṅ* (*çūdrāṇāṁ*) *jātiḥ*, the caste of the Çūdra's.

tarati + *nāuṣ* = *tarati nāuḥ*, the ship crosses.

Treatment of -*s* and -*ṣ* before sibilants:

nṛpas + *sīdati* = *nṛpaḥ sīdati* or *nṛpas sīdati*, the king sits.

cakṣuṣ + *sphurati* = *cakṣuḥ sphurati* or *cakṣus sphurati*, the eye twitches.

bālas + *çete* = *bālaḥ çete* or *bālaç çete*, the boy is lying (on a couch &c.).

khadyotās + *ṣaṭpadāç ca* = *khadyotāḥ ṣaṭpadāç ca* or *khadyotāṣ ṣaṭpadāç ca*, fire-flies and bees.

Change of -*ṣ* to -*r* before voiced consonants:

agniṣ + *dahati* = *agnir dahati*, the fire burns.

sādhuṣ + *yacchati* = *sādhur yacchati*, the good man gives.

nāuṣ + *badhyate* = *nāur badhyate*, the ship is being bound.

Change of -*ṣ* to -*r* before vowels:

ṛṣiṣ + *uvāca* = *ṛṣir uvāca*, the sage said.

viṣṇuṣ + *iva* = *viṣṇur iva*, as Vishnu.

gireṣ + *upatyakā* = *girer upatyakā*, the land lying at the foot of the mountain.

gāuṣ + *iyam* = *gāur iyam*, this cow.

Change of -*iṣ* and -*uṣ* to -*ī* and -*ū* before *r*-:

dāçarathiṣ + *rāmas* = *dāçarathī rāmaḥ*, Rāma, the son of Daçaratha.

çiçuṣ + *roditi* = *çiçū roditi*, the child weeps.

Change of -*as* to -*o* before voiced consonants:

açvas + *dhāvati* = *açvo dhāvati*, the horse runs.

mṛgas + *mriyate* = *mṛgo mriyate*, the antilope dies.

Change of -*as* to -*o* before *a*-:

tuṣṭas + *aham* = *tuṣṭo'ham*, I am satisfied (pleased).

yas + *anṛtaṁ vadati* = *yo'nṛtaṁ vadati*, who speaks untruth.

Change of -*as* to -*a* before other vowels than *a*-:

kāulikas + *āha* = *kāulika āha*, the weaver said.

lomaças + *uvāca* = *lomaça uvāca*, Lomaça said.

Change of *-ās* to *-ā* before voiced consonants and before vowels:

vihagās + *ḍayante* = *vihagā ḍayante*, the birds fly.

narās + *vadanti* = *narā vadanti*, the men say.

bālās + *annam pṛcchanti* = *bālā annam pṛcchanti*, the children ask food.

In particular we must notice the treatment of the pronouns *sa*, that, and *eṣa*, this. Though originally they do not end in *-s*, yet their pausa-form is *saḥ*, *eṣaḥ* and before *a-* they appear as *so*, *eṣo*, after the *-o* of which forms the initial *a-* disappears.

Examples:

sa + *dadarça* = *sa dadarça*, he saw.

sa + *pumān* = *sa pumān*, that man.

sa + *avadat* = *so'vadat*, he said.

mūrkhas + *sa* = *mūrkhaḥ saḥ*, he is a fool.

The exclamation *bhoṣ* before vowels and before voiced consonants appears as *bho* (instead of **bhor*): the cause of this irregularity is the origin of the word, which is a contracted form of *bhavas*, voc. of *bhavant-*, your honor (pron. pers. used in reverent allocution).

§ 110. **Treatment of -r.** The sandhi-rules concerning *-r* are but partly the organic result of phonetic processes: much in the sandhi of *-r* is due to analogy. I shall simply give an account of the rules without trying to trace them to their origin.

Before *c-* (*ch-*) the *-r* is turned into *-ç*; before *ṭ-* (*ṭh-*) into *-ṣ*; before *t-* (*th-*) into *-s*. Before *k* (*kh*), *p* (*ph*), before sibilants and in pausa the *-r* becomes visarga. Before an initial *r-* the final *-r* disappears after lengthening a preceding short vowel. In any other case *-r* remains unchanged.

Substitution of sibilants for *r* before *c-* (*ch-*), *ṭ-*, *t-*:

punar + *cacāra* = *punaç cacāra*, again he wandered.

nisedur + *chāyāyām* = *niṣeduç chāyāyām*, they sat down in the shadow.

pitur + *ṭaṅkas* = *pituṣ ṭaṅkaḥ*, the father's pickaxe.

ūcur + *te* = *ūcus te*, they said.

Change of *-r* to visarga before *k* (*kh*), *p* (*ph*), sibilants and in pausa (only in pausa the change seems to have been organic, see Brugmann 1, 494):

punar + *karoti* = *punaḥ karoti*, again he (she) does.

dadur + *phalāni* = *daduḥ phalāni*, they have given fruits.

babhūvur + *samāje* = *babhūvuḥ samāje*, they were at the assembly.

vanam + *vicerur* = *vanam viceruḥ*, they wandered through the forest.

Change of *-ur*, *-ar* to *-ū*, *-ā* before *r-*:

ūcur + *rāmam* = *ūcū rāmam*, they said to Rāma.

punar + *rakṣati* = *punā rakṣati*, again he protects.

The unchanged *-r* before voiced consonants and before vowels:

pitar + *dehi* = *pitar dehi*, father (voc.), give.

punar + *jagāma* = *punar jagāma*, again he went.

punar + *āha* = *punar āha*, again he said.

dadur + *annam* = *dadur annam*, they gave food.

§ 111. **Changes of initial consonants.** In § 108 we saw, that *ç-* with a preceding dental combines to *cch*. An initial *ch-* becomes *cch-*, when preceded by a short vowel, the preposition (prefix) *ā* or the prohibitive adverb *mā*. Finally we mention the rule, that an initial *h-* is changed to the aspirate of a preceding media, whether this media is original or a softened tenuis (see § 106).

Change of *ch-* to *cch-*:

āhara + *chattram* = *āhara cchattram*, bring the parasol.

ā + *chāditas* = *ācchāditaḥ*, covered.

Change of *h-* to the aspirate of a preceding media:

pṛthak + *haranti* = *pṛthag gharanti*, they take separately.

tad + *hastas* = *taddhastaḥ*, his hand.

PART IV.

ACCENT.

§ 112. **The accent of the Indogermanic period.** Verner's law (Kuhn's Zeitschr. 23, 97 sqq.) has been an evident proof of the fact, that the Indian stress, as it is handed down to us in some Vedic books and by ancient Indian grammarians, generally fell on the same syllables as in the Indogermanic mother-language. In Indian, Balto-Slavonic and Ur-Germanic the so-called *free* accent prevailed, i. e. that neither by the number of syllables nor by the quantity of any syllable the stress was bound to a certain place. Therefore we must assume, that the accent of the mother-language was also a free one. Concerning the accent of the sentence we may learn from the comparison of the Indogermanic languages, that already in a period of dialectic continuity some conjunctions, the interrogative pronouns, when used as indefinites, the personal pronouns, when not used emphatically or antithetically, in many cases also the vocatives and the verbum finitum in an independent clause were deprived of their stress by the preceding word.

Long before the separation of the Indogermanic dialects

all vowels of so-called toneless syllables were weakened: Strachan (Bezz. Beitr. 14, 173 sqq.) and Kretschmer (Kuhn's Zeitschr. 31, 325 sqq.) have shown, that this rule is not to be restricted to pretonic vowels. Many scholars therefore assume, that the Indogermanic accent of an early period must have been a strong expiratorical one (but cf. Finck, Ueber das verhältnis des baltisch-slavischen nominalaccents zum urindogermanischen, Marburg 1895, 29 sqq.) and that it became less expiratorical or even musical towards the end of the proethnic period.

Now there is no longer any doubt, but that the mother-language had two accents of different quality, one of which is represented by the Sanskrit udātta and the Greek ὀξεῖα, while the other has left its traces in the dissyllabic value of some long vowels in the Vedic dialect, the Greek περισπωμένη and the Lithuanian *schleifton*. See Bezzenberger, Bezz. Beitr. 7, 66 sqq.; Hanssen, Kuhn's Zeitschr. 27, 612 sqq.; Hirt, Idg. forschungen 1, 1 sqq. 195 sqq.

To Hirt we owe an excellent monography on all questions concerning the Indogermanic accentuation (Hirt, Der indogermanische akzent, Strassburg 1895).

§ 113. **Accentual agreement between Sanskrit and Greek.** The liberty of accent, which prevailed in the mother-language, was restricted in Greek by many special rules (see Hirt, Der idg. akzent 24 sqq.). Yet there are many words — dissyllabic and trisyllabic —, which have the same accent in Indian and in Greek.

A few examples will suffice:

skr. *padás*, gr. ποδός, gen. of skr. *pát*, foot, gr. dor. πώς.

skr. *tráyas*, three, gr. τρεῖς, but loc. skr. *triṣú*, cf. gr. τρισί.

skr. *páñca*, five, gr. πέντε, goth. *fimf*.

skr. *dáça*, ten, gr. δέκα, goth. *taíhun.*

skr. *saptá*, seven, gr. ἑπτά.

skr. *aṣṭá(u)*, eight, gr. ὀκτώ.

skr. *ṛ́kṣa-s*, bear, gr. ἄρκτος.

skr. *jámbha-s*, set of teeth, gr. γόμφος.

ved. *dáma-s*, house, gr. δόμος.

skr. *áçva-s*, horse, gr. ἵππος, goth. *aíhwa-.*

skr. *ūrdhvá-s*, high, cf. gr. ὀρθός.

ved. *mīḍhá-(m)*, prize, contest, gr. μισθό-(ς).

skr. *dhūmá-s*, smoke, gr. θῡμός.

skr. *yajñá-s*, sacrifice, gr. ἁγνός.

skr. *çrutá-s*, heard, heard of, gr. κλυτός.

skr. *jñātá-s*, known, gr. γνωτός.

skr. *gurú-ṣ*, heavy, gr. βαρύς.

skr. *svādú-ṣ*, sweet, gr. ἡδύς.

skr. *mádhu*, honey, gr. μέθυ.

skr. *nábhas*, sky, gr. νέφος.

véd. *jánas*, race, gr. γένος.

skr. *mánas*, mind, gr. μένος.

skr. *ándhas*, herb, gr. ἄνθος.

skr. *çrávas*, fame, gr. κλέος.

skr. *sádas*, seat, gr. ἕδος·

ved. *bhárma (n)*, bearing, gr. φέρμα.

ved. *hóma (n)*, pouring, oblation, gr. χεῦμα.

ved. *vásma (n)*, cover, gr. lesb. ϝέμμα.

skr. *pitá*, father, gr. πατήρ, goth. *fadar.*

skr. *devá*, brother in law, gr. δᾱήρ.

skr. *bhrátā*, brother, gr. φρά́τωρ, goth. *brōþar.*

skr. *svásā*, sister, cf. gr. ἔορες.

In trisyllabic words and forms:

skr. *úttara-s*, further, left &c., gr. ὕστερος.

skr. *dúhitar*, gr. θύγατερ, voc. of skr. *duhitá*. daughter, gr. θυγάτηρ.

skr. *svádīyas* neutr., sweeter, gr. ἥδιον.

ved. *aṣṭápāt*, with eight feet or parts, gr. ὀκτώπους.

skr. *pitáras*, fathers, gr. πατέρες.

skr. *janitá*, father, gr. γενετήρ.

ved. *iṣirá-s*, strong, quick &c., gr. ἱερός.

skr. *bahulá-s*, numerous &c., gr. παχυλός.

§ 114. **Accentual agreement between Sanskrit and Germanic.** It may be useful to give some examples of Verner's law, which agree with the accent of the identical Sanskrit words and forms:

skr. *pitá*, father, goth. *fadar*, germ. **fadĕr* from **faþĕr*.

skr. *ātmá* (*n*), breath, soul, os. *āđom*, ohg. *ātum*, germ. **ēđmén-* from **ēþmén-*.

skr. *ketú-ṣ*, brightness, light, beam, banner, goth. *haidus*, germ. **χaiđú-s* from **χaiþú-s*.

skr. *nakhára-s* (*nakhará-s*), nail, claw, ohg. *nagal*, germ. **naγló-s* from **naχló-s*.

skr. *vṛkí*, she-wolf, icel. *ylgr*, germ. **ulγṵí-s* from **ulχṵí-s*.

skr. *snuṣá*, daughter in law, ohg. *snura*, germ. **snuzá* from **snusá*.

skr. *māṁsá-m*, flesh, meat, goth. *mimz*, germ. **mimzó-m* from **mimsó-m* (**mēṁsó-m*).

In the verbal system:

skr. *svāpáyāmi*, I cause to sleep, cf. ohg. *int-swebbiu*: skr. *svápna-s*, icel. *svefn*.

skr. *vavṛtimá*, 1 pers. pl. perf., *vavṛtāná-*, part. perf. med. of the root *vart-*, to turn &c., ags. *wurdon, worden*, ohg. *wurtum, giwortan*: skr. *vártana-m*, vb. noun, *vavárta*, 1. 3. pers. sing. perf., ags. *weorđan, wearđ*, ohg. *werdan, ward*.

skr. *didiçimá*, 1 pers. pl. perf., *didiçáná-*, part. perf. med. of the root *deç-*, to indicate &c., ags. *tigon*, *tigen*, ohg. *zigum*, *gizigan*: skr. *déçana-m*, vb. noun, *didéça*, 1. 3. pers. sing. perf., ags. *téon*, *táh*, ohg. *zihan*, *zēh*.

skr. *jujuṣimá*, 1 pers. pl. perf., *jujuṣāṇá-*, part. perf. med., *juṣāṇá-*, part. aor. med. of the root *joṣ-*, to enjoy, ags. *curon*, *coren*, ohg. *kurum*, *gikoran*: skr. *jóṣaṇa-m*, vb. noun, *jujóṣa*, 1. 3. pers. sing. perf., ags. *céosan*, *céas*, ohg. *kiosan*, *kōs*.

§ 115. **Dissyllabic value of long vowels.** Dissyllabic value of long vowels in Vedic, corresponding to the Greek περισπωμένη and the Lithuanian *schleifton*:

a. Gen. pl., ending in *-ām* (*-aam*), for instance ved. *vṛkām* (*vṛkaam*), cf. gr. θεῶν, lith. *vilkú*, ohg. *wolfo* (goth. *wulfē*).

b. Abl. sing. of *-a-* stems, ending in *-ad* (*-aad*), for instance *vṛkād* (*vṛkaad*), cf. lith. *vilkó*, goth. adv. *þaþrō*.

c. Nom. acc. pl. of *-ā-* stems, ending in *-ās* (*-aas*), for instance *áçvās* (*áçvaas*), cf. lith. nom. pl. *mérgós* and goth. *gibōs*.

d. Nom. pl. of *-a-* stems, ending in *-ās* (*-aas*). This form is not preserved in Greek and Lithuanian. With *vṛkās* (*vṛkaas*) only goth. *wulfōs* may be compared.

There are yet other cases, where long vowels of the Vedic dialect have (resp. may have) the metrical value of two syllables, but here it is of no use to cite them all: it will suffice to refer to Hirt, Idg. forschungen 1, 5 sqq.

§ 116. **Accentuation of texts.** The accentuation is marked only in manuscripts of the Saṁhitā's and some other works belonging to the Veda.

The Indian grammarians distinguish the following accents:

1. *udātta-*, i. e. raised, corresponding to the Greek ὀξεῖα.
2. *anudātta-*, i. e. not raised, corresponding to the Greek βαρεῖα.
3. *svarita-*, see Böhtlingk & Roth. The svarita is nearly

always found on syllables, in which a vowel, be it short or long, is preceded by a *y* or *v* representing an original *i* or *u* with udātta-accent. But there is also a *dependent suarita-*, which falls on all syllables immediately preceded by an udātta, whether in the same or in another word, unless it be followed by a syllable, which bears an udātta or a svarita.

In the hymns of the Ṛgveda the accent is written as follows:

1. The udātta is not marked.

2. The svarita, independent or dependent, is marked by a short perpendicular stroke above.

3. The anudātta, next preceding an udātta or independent svarita, is marked by a short horizontal stroke below.

In the lexicon of Böhtlingk and Roth (also in Böhtlingk's chrestomathy) the udātta is indicated by a small Sanskrit *u* above. In transliteration the udātta is written ⏡, the svarita is written ⏡.

Examples:

vípràsya (the *i* bears the udātta and therefore the *a* of the following syllable has a dependent svarita).

kathám rasä́yà ataraḥ páyäm̐si (the first syllable of *rasä́yà*, though immediately preceded by an udātta, has no dependent svarita, because it is also followed by an udātta).

tanvä̀ (with independent svarita, from *tanúà*).

svàr (with independent svarita, from *súàr*).

nadyàs (with independent svarita, from *nadìàs*).

§ 117. **Enclisis.** The principal rules about enclisis are the following:

1. The vocative is enclitic, except at the beginning of a sentence or a pāda.

2. The verbum finitum is enclitic in an independent clause,

except at the beginning of a sentence or a pāda. In a dependent clause it is accented.

3. Many particles (*ca, vā, u, smu, iva, cid, svid, ha* &c.) are always accentless.

4. Many forms of pronominal stems are always enclitic (*mā, me, nāu, nas, tvā, te, vām, vas* &c.).

Some restrictions and particularities are to be found in Whitney's grammar (§ 314 and § 591 sqq.).

Enclitic vocatives:

tvám agne vratapā́ asi.

nákir indra tvád úttaro.

ā́ tú na indra vṛtrahann | asmā́kam ardhám ā́ gahi.

párvatānaam | khidrám bibharṣi pṛthivi.

But:

ágne yáṁ yajñám adhvarám | viçvátaḥ paribhúr ási.

ágne náya supáthā rāyé asmā́n.

vā́yo yé te sahasríṇo | ráthāsas tébhir ā́ gahi.

yátaḥ pári jārá ivācárantī | úṣo dadṛkṣé ná púnar yatíva.

Enclitic verbum finitum:

índraṁ víçvā avīvṛdhan | samudrávyacasaṁ gíraḥ.

agníṁ dūtáṁ vṛṇīmahe.

parjányāya prá gāyata.

asmé indrā varuṇā çárma yacchatam.

But:

gā́yanti tvā gāyatríṇo | árcanti arkám arkíṇaḥ.

gṛbhṇā́mi te sāubhagatvā́ya hástam.

índrasya nú vīríāṇi prá vocam | yā́ni cakā́ra prathamā́ni vajrī́.

ráthaṁ yé cakrúḥ suvṛ́taṁ nareṣṭhā́m.

yó gárbham óṣadhīnaam | gávāṁ kṛṇóti árvatām.

yā́su (apsú) rā́jā váruṇo yā́su sómaḥ | víçve devā́ yā́su ūrjaṁ mádanti.